COIT TOWER

A NOVEL OF SAN FRANCISCO

Bill Issel

Carleton Street Publications

ISBN: 978-0926664-20-3

Coit Tower is a work of fiction. Names, dialogue, institutions, scenes, interactions, and settings are products of my imagination and should not be taken as statements of facts. Some real historical and public figures, agencies, and events, do appear, but the conversations, incidents, and settings concerning them are fictional, not meant to depict history or alter the fictional nature of the book. Any resemblance to persons living or dead is entirely coincidental.

Book layout and Design: Chris Carlsson

"The truth is rarely pure and never simple."

—Oscar Wilde

Prologue   Sunday, March 29, 1942

anny Wong advertised two shows for Palm Sunday. Both featured the new dancer Lily of the Valley. Her photo, which left little to the imagination, was captioned "Lily's Palm Dance, the one you won't see in Church today."

Harlan Winthrop was enthralled by Lily's dances. The first time she performed at the Cellar Club was last November, when she did "Lily's Thanksgiving Dance, the one you will be grateful for."

He liked that Lily brought such a winning combination of innocence and coquetry to her dances. He smiled as he watched her play the crowd.

Like many others, Harlan purchased photos of Lily that Danny Wong sold for a dollar. She went from table to table after the dance to sign the photos. When she asked him for his name and said out loud as she autographed the photo, "To Harlan, with love, Lily," he felt himself getting aroused.

Harlan was a regular at Danny Wong's place and several other Chinatown clubs. He also liked getting together with his friends to wine and dine at his villa across the bay. They'd gathered there all through Prohibition and now it housed a fine collection of French erotic art and literature. All except for the first editions of *Justine* and *Juliette* by Marquis de Sade. Those books were among Harlan's most precious possessions. He kept them safe in the bookshelf in his bedroom.

On the morning of Palm Sunday he'd seen the Christians, clutching their King James Bibles, flocking like sheep into the

Grace Episcopalian Cathedral. The *Les Amis de Juliette* had no need for it. They lived by the Gospel of de Sade, worshipful graduates of The School of Licentiousness. Proper San Franciscans, Harlan and his friends included young girls from all over the world in their gatherings.

When Lily of the Valley signed his photo at the Lenten Dance, the issue was decided. Harlan would bring Lily to meet *Les Amis* at their next get together. Now, a day later, he quickly made the walk from Aquatic Park to the top of Nob Hill without getting winded. He always prided himself on his athletic physique, thanks to rowing on Lake Merced, golf at the Olympic Club, and swimming at the Dolphin Club.

He entered his Sacramento Street apartment house, went to his bedroom, and changed out of his dungarees and sweater. He had already laid out his outfit for this evening: a bespoke suit of dark gray worsted wool made for him by a tailor in Hong Kong, and a deep red silk shirt, which he would wear with a black silk tie. His black Johnston & Murphy dress shoes were polished.

He decided to shave again. Even into his late forties he maintained the thick black hair and chiseled good looks that had earned him the yearbook sobriquet "Most likely to be leading man with Mary Pickford" in 1915, his graduation year.

Harlan never regretted the move to San Francisco from Boston after his graduation from Princeton. After all, New Englanders had been top dogs in "The Wall Street of the West" since even before the Gold Rush. And he had quickly become part of the Nob Hill and Montgomery Street leadership class. No one was surprised when the mayor asked him to preside over the committee running the city's war bonds campaign.

After dressing and drinking a glass of bourbon, which he enjoyed straight, he left his apartment, walked to his garage, and unlocked his car. He knew from experience that elegant young women enjoyed riding in his new Packard Super Eight 160 station wagon.

He found a parking space only a half block from Danny Wong's place. He locked the car and walked to his club for dinner. He would walk back to Chinatown for the second show, and when it ended he would invite Lily to meet his cosmopolitan friends.

The front page stories in the Sunday *San Francisco Examiner* he picked up after dinner at the club threatened to spoil his mood. The paper was full of news about the expanding war in the Pacific. The Japanese were taking the Solomon Islands. *Never mind, he thought, with Stalin and the Soviet Union on our side now, the Japanese and their Axis partners will never defeat us.* He put the paper away, sipped his Courvoisier and fantasized about an evening at the villa with Lily of the Valley.

Chapter 1   Monday, March 30, 1942

I was lighting my first Lucky Strike of the morning, enjoying the view of the Golden Gate Bridge beyond the Marina, when the telephone rang. I put my cigarette in the ashtray and picked up.

"Hello, this is Tony Bosco."

"Tony, this is Chief O'Reilly," said the voice on the other end, an unmistakable mix of County Kerry brogue and San Francisco waterfront.

"Chief," I said, "what brings you to call me from the Second and Third Circles of Hell down there next door to Chinatown and the Barbary Coast?"

"I'm afraid the reason for my call is no laughing matter," O'Reilly said.

"You used to enjoy my allusions to Dante when I was on the Police Commission."

"Maybe so, but we're at war now. I'm sure you don't have a party line there in Pacific Heights, but I don't want to talk about this on the telephone," he said. "I'm hoping you can come down to the Hall of Justice so we can talk in person."

"This sounds serious. I was going to do some paperwork at home this morning, but I can come to the Hall of Justice instead."

"All right," the chief replied. "The sooner the better." The phone clicked in my ear.

The Gerald O'Reilly I've known all these years would never hang up without saying goodbye. What had gotten into him?

I put out my smoldering cigarette and went to get ready for the day.

The three-piece blue suit I had worn to Palm Sunday Mass yesterday was still hanging on my valet stand. I took a fresh laundered white shirt from the closet and a tie with a green and brown paisley design.

"Tony," my wife said when I walked into the kitchen, "I love you in that tie. It brings out the green in your hazel eyes and complements your brown hair." She came over to me, reached up, mussed my hair, and hugged me. "But why are you dressed in your blue suit? I thought you were going to be working in your study this morning."

She went back to the stove to assemble the espresso coffee-maker. She put the top and bottom of the pot together as I told her about the chief's call. "We haven't seen Chief O'Reilly since he and his wife came for dinner, just before Christmas," she said. "I wonder what's happening?" She turned on the gas under the coffee pot. "I was about to bring a cup of espresso to you in your study. Would you like it now before you leave?"

"Thank you, Flora, but I better go directly down to the Hall of Justice," I replied. "It sounded urgent." I kissed her goodbye, took a navy blue Stetson fedora off the hat rack by the front door and went outside.

My 1940 Buick Century was parked outside on Filbert Street. I made a U-turn, headed downtown then turned left onto Divisadero to Broadway and right on Broadway down to the Hall of Justice on Kearny Street.

I love my "banker's hot rod." It's powerful, comfortable, and its black finish gleams in the sunshine and glows in the reflection of the streetlights at night. The three kids hanging out by the entrance to the Salesian Boy's Club next to the Italian Cathedral whistled and waved to me as I drove past. Maybe they thought I was Amadeo or Mario Giannini from the Bank of America.

Charlie O'Brien walked up to the car after I parked it in the garage next to his office. He looked like he was wearing the same extra-large greasy coveralls he wore when I was on the Police Commission four years ago.

"Commissioner," he said in his gravelly voice, "we haven't seen you for a while. When did you trade your Chevy workhorse for this Buick stallion? I'd shake your hand, but I'm dirty as usual."

I put out my hand and grabbed his. "Charlie, it's good to see you. I bought this beauty two years ago." The familiar scent — a distinctive mélange of motor oil, gasoline, cigarette smoke and sweat — reminded me how much I missed my time on the Commission when the Hall of Justice was my second home and I was a regular at Charlie's Portsmouth Square Garage.

"How have you been?" I asked. "Are you still living out on 20th Street? The last I recall, your son just started St. James High School."

"You have a great memory," Charlie said. "Yeah, we're still out in the Mission. Patrick is doing well. His mother's not happy he decided on high school instead of the junior seminary, but frankly I'm just as glad he's not going to be a priest. We have enough of those holy rollers already."

"I get you, Charlie. We have too many bad priests. We can use more good ones. But if your Patrick doesn't have a vocation, he's right to go to St. James instead of the seminary."

"I agree," Charlie said. "Anyhow the family's fine. I appreciate you asking about them. So, what brings you down here today?"

"Well, I haven't seen my pals at the Hall of Justice for a while," I said, remembering that the chief was wary about discussing the matter on the phone. "And it's Holy Week, right?" I smiled at him and chuckled. "They might need some spiritual advice down here next door to the Barbary Coast."

Charlie laughed. "In that case, I guess I better wash your Buick with holy water."

"*Ego te absolvo*," I joked, making the sign of the cross over him as if he were my parishioner. I handed over the keys to my Century. "Take care of my thoroughbred, my friend. I'll be back for him in a couple of hours."

I walked across Portsmouth Square to the Hall of Justice. Some old Chinese men and women were sitting on the benches scattering pieces of bread on the ground. At least a dozen pigeons swooped down and began to fight each other over the bread. Little groups of sailors in uniform sat together, smoking and talking and passing around a flask. When the Chinatown souvenir stores opened at 11:00 they would be walking up to Grant Avenue to buy tiny porcelain vases and brightly colored little dolls to send to their families back home in Nebraska and North Dakota.

I greeted Inspector Leo Brennan as I walked into the Hall. He was on his way out, wearing his usual uniform — gray suit and spring weight topcoat and a black hat, tipped to one side in a rakish angle.

A half dozen kids who couldn't have been more than twelve or thirteen were standing alongside the usual crowd of uniformed officers, detectives, and down-at-the-heel would-be informers. The kids all had bicycles. The porter, a retired cop in his seventies who everybody calls Seamus told me they were part of the Junior Victory Army. "They were just sworn in by the Deputy Chief and will be riding back and forth between the Hall of Justice and Fort

Mason delivering messages to the Army brass out there."

The war was changing the city. Armed guards were patrolling the Golden Gate Bridge, sandbags covering the windows on the ground floor of the City Hall. A servicemen's hospitality center was doing business in the park next to the Civic Center. The other afternoon, the *Call Bulletin* printed a photograph showing Inspector Brennan arresting Genzo Nakaharo at his bakery in Japantown.

I opened the chief's door and greeted his secretary, Maggie McPherson, who looked up at me from her desk with a concerned expression.

"Commissioner Bosco," she said. "The chief was not expecting you until this afternoon but I know he'll be glad to see you. I don't know what the matter is, but he is in a state! I've never seen him like this."

Just then, the door to the chief's office opened and Gerald O'Reilly said, "Tony, I am glad to see you. Come inside." He looked tired and had a few new worry lines in his face. His uniform seemed too big on his stocky frame. He must have lost some weight since I saw him four months ago.

When he opened the door wider to make room for me to enter, I saw another visitor standing in front of the chief's desk.

"I don't think you know Detective Sullivan," O'Reilly said. "He's a newcomer to the department, but his family has deep roots in San Francisco."

A strong looking man in his late twenties, with piercing black eyes that looked larger than normal because of his steel rimmed glasses, Sullivan parted his thick black hair on the left in a pompadour. He observed me with an intent expression, took a couple of steps forward and held out his large right hand. "Dennis Sullivan," he said in a confident voice that matched his large frame.

I figured he was at least twenty years younger, and he towered over me. Maybe six-foot-three with a forty-four size suit and seventeen-inch collar. "You don't know me from Adam, but I know who you are. You're famous at St. Mary's. Nobody else ever won the College medals in Rhetoric, Latin, and French *and* captained the Gaels for *two* championships!"

"That's all true," I said. "I don't believe in false modesty. But tell me about yourself."

"I graduated in the same class as Joe Alioto."

"I know Joe, of course," I replied. "He's been active in our Catholic Men's organization."

"Joe went east to law school at the Catholic University, but I signed up here at USF," Dennis said. "Then I spent over a year traveling through the United Kingdom and Europe. I wanted to see for myself what was going on in Ireland, Germany, and Italy."

"That's a lot of traveling," I said. "Did you manage to get an audience with the Pope when you went to Italy?"

"No," he said, "but I did get to meet Éamon de Valera when I was in Dublin."

"Lucky you. I'd like to shake the hand of the man who wrote Catholic values into the Constitution of Ireland."

A frown came over Sullivan's face. "He's an impressive man, Commissioner, but I prefer our American constitution. Separation of church and state and all that."

"Hmm." I found myself gently grabbing the younger man's shoulder. "Getting the right morals into our public life, that's the thing, don't you think?"

Sullivan nodded. "Sure. I agree with that. Actually, I'd like to be in uniform right now defending us against the Axis, but when I tried to enlist the day after Pearl Harbor, the Army made me 4-F on account of my eyesight. I appealed, but no dice."

"I'm sorry to hear that," I said.

He shrugged. "I applied to the SFPD and got accepted right away. I'm the first detective on the force with a college degree and a law degree. They made me a detective right away because they have a shortage with so many of the regular guys already gone to fight Tojo and Hitler."

"Well," said the chief, "your performance on the written and physical exams, and your football and swimming medals from St. Mary's didn't hurt your application, either. Not to mention the fact everybody knows about your Uncle John's record as assistant district attorney during the Graft Trials, and your Uncle Patrick's heroism in the fire department during the Big Quake back in '06."

He made a sign for us to have a seat.

"But I didn't call you two here to discuss pedigrees," he said. "You both know we have deep divisions in this city. People are anxious because of the war. Many of them feel torn between their American patriotism and their Italian, German, and Japanese ancestral ties."

"I don't know if you saw the article about Inspector Brennan's arrest of that Jap baker, but I don't like this kind of story. The reporters are looking for scoops, playing up how the police department is a bunch of nasty coldhearted characters when we're just doing our job."

He held up a copy of *The People's World*. "These communists are the worst." He let the paper drop on his desk with a look of disgust.

"I called you here because now we have an even worse situation. I want your help in dealing with it and making sure the press and the public never hear a word about it."

Sullivan and I locked eyes. He looked as confused as me.

"Yesterday was Palm Sunday," the chief said. "The three of us were probably at Mass, but somebody else was murdering one of our leading citizens. He broke into Coit Tower, where he dumped the body and marked up the wall with what must be some kind of war-related message."

The chief got up from his desk and stood in front of it. He ran his fingers through his already wild-looking hair.

"This morning the caretaker discovered the body with a dagger stuck in its back, sprawled on the floor next to that mural showing a man taking a book by Karl Marx from a library shelf."

I started to say something but the chief held up his hand. "Hold on, it gets worse. Somebody defaced the mural. They wrote RoBerTo in white paint below the shelf with the Karl Marx book."

"Oh my God," Sullivan said. "That's the code word Mussolini lovers use when they greet each other to signify their support for an Axis victory: Ro for Rome, Ber for Berlin, To for Tokyo — Ro-BerTo."

I nodded. "I know that mural. The archbishop tried to get Mayor Rossi to paint over the Karl Marx book and the Red newspapers to no avail."

The chief continued, "The caretaker called the police. Two officers from the Central Station drove up there to take a look. They reported back to their captain and he called me right away. I told him to have the officers stand guard at the door and let nobody in or out. I told our press officer to tell any reporters who call that we closed Coit Tower for emergency repairs."

"So, who is the victim?" I asked.

"Harlan Winthrop," the chief said, almost in a whisper. "His face looked gray, almost white. His eyes were wide open."

He sat back down, put his elbows on the desk and folded his hands.

"I noticed when I first saw him that there was no blood on the floor. That means the killer stabbed him somewhere else, let him bleed out, and then dumped him on the floor in Coit Tower before painting the message on the wall."

I found myself speechless. I knew Harlan for years, back to when he supported our North Beach campaign for an official city celebration of Columbus Day. He was president of the San Francisco Chamber of Commerce at the same time I was president of the Italian Chamber of Commerce.

"This is terrible, Chief," I said. "You and I both got along with Harlan despite our political differences." I turned to Dennis. "We're Democrats and supported President Roosevelt and he was a Herbert Hoover Republican who thought Roosevelt was a traitor to his class."

"Who do you think could have done such a thing?" Dennis asked.

"I don't know what to think," O'Reilly replied, his tired voice matching his drawn features. "What I do know is that the police department can't afford this, whatever it is. We are already getting too much bad press for arresting real Jap spies. God knows what they are going to say about us when we help the Army move all the Jap families out of the city next week."

Dennis shook his head and frowned. He looked at me like he expected me to say something, but I kept a straight face and stayed silent.

"I have already sworn to secrecy the caretaker, the captain of Central Station, the officers who first arrived at the scene, and the coroner," the chief said. "I told them that if this gets into the papers, I will fire them all. I'm determined to keep the news of this murder from the press and the public. I'm worried about the city.

"People are nervous about the air raid scares, and nobody knows for sure whether the Japanese will invade California."

"I can just imagine how the public would react if they read a headline in the *San Francisco Chronicle* 'Police Search for the RoBerTo murderer'," Sullivan said.

The chief nodded. "If people think that a murderer is on the loose — an Italian, German, or Japanese terrorist — we'll have an impossible situation on our hands."

"The Germans had secret agents working out of their residence in the Whittier Mansion in Pacific Heights," Sullivan said, "but the consul and his family and all of them left San Francisco the day after the president closed all of those consulates in the whole country."

"That's right," the chief said, "they've been gone more than eight months. Besides, we never had a big pro-Hitler German outfit here like the one in Yorkville in New York City."

"What about the Japs?" Sullivan asked. "Could one of those Dragon societies that had demonstrations and parades in Japantown have ordered this murder?"

"We better consider that possibility," the chief replied, "but J. Edgar Hoover has been on top of those emperor worshippers since long before Pearl Harbor. The FBI has agents out here doing surveillance on all of those they call 'potentially subversive' Japs."

He looked at me. "The same thing goes for the Italians," he said. "Tony, I'm sorry to say you are on that list, but it's nothing to worry about."

I laughed. I knew all about Hoover's list. "Hoover has probably been tracking everyone who did work for the Italian consulate. But there are so many of us that the feds can't watch us all."

I took out my Lucky Strikes and lit up. "If word gets out about this, the longer it takes to find the killer, the more the police department will be criticized for failing to do its duty," I said. "I was on the Police Commission during the Atherton Investigation. You know how we were vilified in the papers: corrupt, incompetent, in league with the very criminals we were supposed to be fighting against."

"We can't let that happen again," the chief said. "I'm delegating the two of you to find the killer, figure out if he's part of something bigger, and — especially — keep this whole thing quiet. You report to me and only me. I'll give you an office in the basement. If anybody asks you what you're doing, tell them I asked you to work together to improve communication between the SFPD and General Dewitt's headquarters at Fort Mason."

Sullivan and I looked at each other. "You can count on me, Chief," I said.

"That goes for me too," Sullivan added.

"Maggie doesn't know anything about this. Let's go tell her about your 'communication' job. Then she can set you up in an office."

I nodded. "Then Dennis and I will go check out the crime scene," I said. "If this is a murder by a pro-Axis terrorist, then Coit Tower's a new front in the war."

Chapter 2   Monday, March 30, 1942

aggie walked downstairs with us. When we got to the basement, she took us to a door with a frosted glass window marked No Admittance. "This is where we used to store guns the department confiscated from the bad guys," she explained. "Hundreds and hundreds of them piled up on the shelves and in big wooden boxes. But we cleaned it out and sent each and every revolver, pistol, shotgun, and rifle — even some tommy guns — to Fort Mason as part of the scrap iron for victory program."

She unlocked the door and we went inside.

The room was about ten feet by twelve. Empty, unfinished wooden shelves lined two of the four walls. A light fixture hung from the ceiling. It came on when I pulled on a string with a brass washer at the end. The shelves were dusty and so was the floor. "I can get a partner's desk, a desk lamp, and a couple of desk chairs for you," Maggie said. "Do you need a file cabinet, too?"

"We don't need a file cabinet," I answered, "but we need the place cleaned up. Please get a janitor down here today so we can begin using the room tomorrow." I looked around. "I don't see a telephone. We will need one right away, so do what you can to have us hooked up as soon as possible. We are supposed to be improving communications; we can't do that without a telephone."

Maggie chuckled.

"Come to think of it," I said, "let's get two telephones, each with its own number."

"Will do," Maggie said. "I guess I should also order the painters to replace the sign with your names and 'Communication Office'."

I locked eyes with Dennis and shook my head. "No need. We are at war, we need to conserve manpower and paint."

Maggie turned to me and gave me two keys to the room. "Is there anything else you'd like me to do, Commissioner?" she asked. "If not, I will leave you to it and go back upstairs to order your telephones and furniture."

"Thanks, Maggie," Dennis said.

"It's good to be working with you again," I added.

She smiled and left the room. We could hear her high heels clicking on the marble floor as she made her way to the stairway.

I turned to Dennis. "We can't do anything here today. We need to go to Coit Tower." I looked at my watch. "But since it's about lunch time, let's get ourselves something to eat first."

Outside on Kearny Street, we found ourselves surrounded by the hustle and bustle that was now an everyday reality in downtown San Francisco. "I can't get used to how much more crowded the city is," I said to Dennis. "I guess we can blame all this congestion on the Japs."

"It's not all the fault of the Japs," Dennis replied. "If you mean the attack on Pearl Harbor. The Army started expanding the Fort Mason embarkation facilities even before last year, and the Navy took over the ship repair yard down at Hunters Point a couple of years ago.

"When I got home just over a year ago, I was amazed at how much more crowded the city got during my eighteen months in Europe."

I sighed. "I guess you're right, but it's much worse now."

"No question," he replied.

Portsmouth Square was packed with clusters of young servicemen in Army and Navy uniforms. Several groups of girls dressed in the latest fashion of tight sweaters, skirts, white bobby sox, loafers and saddle shoes busied themselves in animated conversation with some of the sailors.

"Those girls must be cold," Dennis remarked. "And they don't look old enough to have graduated from high school yet."

"Maybe you are paying more attention to those girls than you should," I said with a wink.

He laughed. "Maybe I like a different kind of Catholic Action than you do."

We were both laughing as we crossed the street and passed the McDonough Bail Bond office. Kearny Street was crowded with people. You could tell that many of them were newcomers, young men and women in their early twenties wearing heavy coats made for icy winters back east, not our lightweight Bay Area models better suited to this blustery but sunny day.

"Do you like Vanessi's?" I asked.

"Sure, who doesn't," Dennis replied, "but I can't afford to eat lunch there. I usually have a sandwich and a cup of coffee at Fosters or Compton's Cafeteria."

I put a hand on his shoulder. "Don't worry, it's my treat. We must raise a glass in memory of Harlan Winthrop and mark the beginning of — what? Shall we, in the spirit of the chief's charge to us, call it a campaign?"

Dennis started to reply, but he was drowned out by the piercing noise of a loud bell and the metallic clatter of a Number 29 streetcar that passed us on its way down Kearny to Market Street.

"Before that Iron Monster came by, I was going to ask you if we shouldn't first go up to Coit Tower to see the crime scene," he said.

"Well, Vanessi's is on the way, if you don't mind walking. Harlan is not going anywhere. Unless, of course, you don't want to view the body after lunch." I smiled. "But you don't impress me as being a guy with a weak stomach."

Just as we started to cross Broadway, we had to jump back to avoid getting hit by the cow catcher of another white-front streetcar. The thing speeded up instead of putting on the brake as it came toward us. I had to resist the temptation to shout out a reprimand to the motorman for his reckless driving.

"My God," Dennis exclaimed. "What was that guy trying to prove?"

"For years, but especially since the General Strike in '34, these streetcar operators and conductors have brazenly acted out their hostility and discourtesy toward anyone wearing a suit and a tie," I explained. "The city should do something, but the mayor and the Board of Supervisors lack the courage to go up against the unions. I support Roosevelt's putting our government on the side of working people with his New Deal, but there's no getting around the fact that unions are abusing their new powers."

"I don't know about that," Dennis said. "Isn't that one of those glittering generalities that the Christian Brothers at St. Mary's warned us against?"

I sighed. "I guess you're right. I'm fifty-three now, and find myself getting more conservative and judgmental. And vain!"

Dennis chuckled.

"Maybe that motorman was just having a good time scaring

the devil out of a couple of guys dressed in expensive suits he could never afford," I said. "Who knows, he might not even like unions. For all I know, he might resent having to pay his union dues every week. I better be careful, or I'll start to feel guilty for getting angry at..."

"That SOB," Dennis said decisively, and we both laughed hard as we crossed the street to the restaurant.

With its distinctive Art Deco oval windows and a red awning with its name in gold letters extending from the building to the curb, Vanessi's attracted customers from all over the city. Still chuckling, we moved from the corner toward the concrete stairs cut into the steep sidewalk of Kearny as it goes uphill to Vallejo, so the three men who were leaving the restaurant could pass us.

I was about to walk toward the awning when I noticed the men had stopped.

"What's so funny, *consigliere*?" sneered a hatless swarthy thin-faced man with wavy brown hair wearing a rumpled brown suit. He was now standing less than a foot from me, face to face. "Did you get permission from the archbishop to laugh in public?"

The smoke from the cigarette he was holding in his right hand was drifting into the space between our faces and getting in my eyes.

"Signor Sarno," I replied, "I wouldn't have imagined you frequented Vanessi's. After all, Pietro and Mary Nicoletti will put a tenth of your money into the collection basket at Saints Peter and Paul church on Sunday."

Sarno grinned. "I didn't pay for my lunch. I was the guest of these two gentlemen."

"How nice for you," I replied. "And are you going to introduce us? I will even provide you with a model of good manners, which as usual you seem to require."

I made a gesture toward Dennis. "Mr. Eddie Sarno, this is *Detective* Dennis Sullivan, of the San Francisco Police Department. He's a graduate of my alma mater St. Mary's College and the University of San Francisco Law School."

Eddie dropped his cigarette, which had burned down to the end, and stubbed it out on the sidewalk. "How do you do, *Detective.* Pardon me if I don't say it's a pleasure to meet you. I don't like to pretend that I believe the cops are on the side of the people."

He turned toward the two men. "Now Quid pro quo, consigliere," he mocked. "Let me introduce two gentlemen who are very much on the side of the people. In fact, they are both associated with *The People's World* which, as you may remember from the articles that have featured you, actually tells the people the truth, as opposed to those capitalist rags like the *Examiner* and *The Chronicle.*

"This is Al Richmond, the editor of PW and Mike Quinn, one of his best writers."

Dennis and I shook hands with Richmond and Quinn. I put my hand to my hat, nodded, and said, "Gentlemen," then made the V for Victory sign. Richmond and Quinn nodded back and returned my Victory salutation. Sarno turned on his heel without a word and they all crossed Kearny, walking up Broadway toward Columbus Avenue.

Once inside the restaurant, Dennis and I gave our hats to Muriel, the red-haired Irish girl with peaches and cream complexion who worked in the cloak room. She handed us two paper claim tickets.

"Hello, Commissioner Bosco," she said, her light blue eyes sparkling as she looked from me to Dennis Sullivan. "We are always happy to see you. And I see you have a new friend. Aren't you going to introduce us?"

"Muriel, this is Dennis Sullivan, a new detective down at the Hall of Justice. He and I are improving communications between the chief and General DeWitt. Say hello, but don't go distracting him from his important defense job."

Muriel blushed beet red, a color that clashed with the rusty hue of her long wavy hair, but she didn't miss a beat. "I wouldn't think of distracting this serious-looking young gentleman," she said. "Unless, of course, he asked me nicely." She turned away to put our hats in the cloakroom.

Dennis and I walked into the restaurant and took two empty seats at the counter. Mario Moretti, wearing his starched chef's toque, had his back to us as he broiled a couple of steaks. On the range to his left several pots of spaghetti and linguini were boiling away. Clean dishes of various sizes were stacked on the shelves above the six-burner range. Two plates of steak and pasta sat on the warming shelf above the broiler, ready to be delivered to customers.

Before we could say hello to Mario, Pietro walked over and greeted us. I introduced Dennis and couldn't resist mentioning that I saw Eddie Sarno leaving here with a couple of Reds. "When did you start consorting with the enemy?" I asked.

He frowned. "Commissioner, you've known me for a long time, since way before I opened this place in '36. You know everybody's money is good at Vanessi's. Besides, we're allies now, right? Fighting Hitler and Mussolini. Me, I'm happy to serve all of the fellow fighters against fascism and Nazism in my little restaurant."

"Okay, okay, Pietro, don't get hot under the collar. I was needling you. I believe that everybody is innocent until they are proven guilty, right? But you have to admit, Sarno is not tolerant like you are. He's attacked me in his paper so many times I've lost count. And with the most outrageous lies and personal insults. You can't blame me if I have a hard time tolerating a guy like him. The same goes for *The People's World*. They say that A.P Giannini and the mayor and I are all fascist devils secretly working for Mussolini and Hitler."

"I know, you are right," Pietro said. "I told him and his Commie pals a long time ago that they shouldn't have called you and Mayor Rossi *agenti fascisti* during the last election. Nobody believes that stuff. But, c'mon, Tony, that's politics. You gotta admit that you guys didn't exactly talk all lovey dovey about the Commie candidates either."

"I'm surprised you would defend him like this, Pietro," I said.

"Well counselor, Eddie, he had a hard life — a poor kid growing up in a slum in Napoli. I heard the priests and the nuns in the orphanage he lived in beat him up so bad he ran away. I think we should give him a break.

"Anyway, he means well. He's on the side of the little people. It's not his fault that the only Church people he knew treated him bad. You have to go easy on him, counselor. He didn't get to go to a good high school like Sacred Heart and a good college like St. Mary's."

I sighed. "I should probably ease up on Eddie. And maybe you're right that nobody believes the lies that him and his Red friends are printing."

Dennis leaned forward. "I've been quiet here, but it does seem like every newsstand now has copies of *The People's World* and *Il Corriere del Populo.* Whenever I'm on a streetcar somebody is reading one of those papers. That never used to happen."

Pietro put up his hands and said, "Maybe you will feel better if I tell you that the other day Eddie was here having lunch with Special Agent Piper — you know, from the FBI office. We are all on the same side now, and we have to let bygones be bygones."

"I'm happy to oblige," I answered. "But tell Sarno the same thing, will you? He just insulted me again outside so maybe he hasn't gotten the word yet." I turned to Dennis. "Now let's order, I'm ready for a plate of the best Brasato al Barolo in North Beach."

"What about you, Detective?" asked Pietro. "What will you have?"

Dennis smiled. "How about a steak, since he's treating. I like it well done."

"And bring us a bottle of Barbera d'Asti," I said. "I know you stocked up on it when that idiot Mussolini let himself be photographed kowtowing to Hitler."

As we waited for our wine, newly arrived customers lined up behind us, waiting for empty seats.

Pietro arrived with the wine, and I turned to him. "Imagine, sitting here in California drinking the wine of my hometown while our American boys with Italian parents and grandparents have to get ready to fight to free Italy from fascism. What a world!"

Pietro shook his head in agreement, uncorked the wine, poured two glasses for us, and left to talk with other customers.

"I never heard all that stuff about what happened during the election," Dennis said. "I was traveling in Europe then."

"You missed a rip roaring campaign," I replied. "But Pietro is right. We were as nasty to the Reds as they were to us. We put up billboards showing what Mayor Rossi's opponent Franck Havenner would do if he won the election — paint the City Hall dome red! Well, we won and Franck lost, but he's not a Commie at all."

I took a drink of my Barbera. "But we weren't as bad as Eddie's pal, Al Richmond — who I bet you ten dollars is a New York Jew by the look of him — who attacked me for being 'an Italian Aryan.'"

"Jeez, Tony," Dennis said, a shocked look on his face. "I'm surprised to hear you talking like this! I never would have imagined you to be anti-Semitic. Professor Hennessy would jump all over you if he heard you using such language."

I felt myself getting hot all over. "I guess I'm more upset about all this than I realized. You're right. There's no excuse for using such language. My wife has also reminded me that I sometimes sound like Father Coughlin."

"Pietro says that Eddie Sarno is having lunch with an FBI agent, so he must be helping our government," Dennis said.

"And I heard that Eddie got his citizenship papers, so maybe I should give him a chance to prove he's really an American patriot."

"Yeah," Dennis replied.

I gave him a cold smile. "But we lawyers all know that the real truth of the matter is you're always guilty until proven innocent."

Chapter 3   **Monday, March 30, 1942**

"**D**ennis, would you like one?" I asked, taking the pack of Luckies out of the inside pocket of my suit.

He shook his head. "I don't smoke. When I was about thirteen, I stole a Camel from my dad and lit up with one of my friends. I hated the taste of it and I haven't been tempted since. Besides, Coach O'Leary at St. Mary's told us horror stories of what smoking can do to wreck your wind."

"I remember O'Leary, and I won't ask you again, but you don't need to make me feel guilty," I said. "My wife is always telling me she hates the smell of cigarettes and cigars. Mea Culpa, Mr. Athlete."

Dennis laughed. "Tony, you don't need to feel guilty. I don't mind if you smoke. Everybody else in here seems to be doing it."

Pietro came over and asked, "Are you gentlemen having dessert? Commissioner, I know you like our Zabaglione, made with Moscato d'Asti from your home town. Shall I ask Mario to whip up two cups for you?"

"Not today, Pietro," I answered. "We have to get back to work." He brought the check and I handed him three one dollar bills. "Keep the change," I said. We exchanged V for Victory signs and said, "*Buona Sera.*"

Another hatcheck girl was at Muriel's station. She was in her thirties, tall and thin with short brown hair. She had red-rimmed eyes like she had been crying. I noticed she was wearing a wedding ring. When we took our hats and put a dime in the tip dish, she just nodded, her thin lips compressed in a frown.

"What a difference from Muriel," Dennis commented. "From sunshine to a rainy day."

"We shouldn't judge," I said. "Maybe one of the men in her family just went to war, or she heard some bad news."

"Yeah," Dennis agreed, "but you have to admit, Muriel's good humor was distracting. After talking to the chief I was glad to be distracted for a few minutes."

"That is for sure," I said as we started walking up the stairs in the sidewalk on Kearny Street and headed up the hill.

Three sailors, with red faces and loud voices, their arms around each other's shoulders, were walking down the middle of the steep street. As they passed us, one of them pulled a flask from the pocket of his tight-fitting pants and held it out to me. "How about a drink, grandpop?" They all guffawed and continued down the hill.

There's not much traffic on this block of Kearny, it's too steep, but nobody used to walk in the street the way the servicemen did now.

"I have a feeling the city's never going to be the same after this war," I said to Dennis.

The walk to Coit Tower was all uphill. By the time we got there, I was reminded of Dennis' comment about how smoking wrecked your wind. The two officers guarding the front door let us in after Dennis showed his badge, and we walked upstairs to the caretaker's apartment on the second floor. Dennis knocked on the door. Almost immediately, it was opened by a tall ramrod-straight man in his sixties. He had a Clark Gable mustache and said in a strict-sounding but not unfriendly voice, "You must be the police."

"I'm Police Commissioner Tony Bosco and this is Detective Dennis Sullivan," I said. "Chief O'Reilly has delegated us to investigate Harlan Winthrop's murder."

"I'm Lieutenant Colonel Bob Brody," the man replied. "I'm the caretaker." We shook hands. "Step inside, will you," he said, "and let me brief you on what I know."

He gestured to a nervous-looking petite woman in her fifties who was drying her hands on a dishtowel. "This is my wife, Marion," he said. The woman made a brief bow to the two of us before going back into the kitchen at the end of the entry hall.

Brody took us into a small living room where we all sat down. "I told Marion what I discovered but I will not let her see the dead body next to the 'Library' mural," he said. "I'd appreciate it if you could respect the fact that she is a lady and not trouble her with the awful details. She already had to go through the embarrassing experience of having to walk back and forth past a mural with a naked boy going swimming. We finally got it painted over, but it was shocking to her."

"The chief said that Harlan's body is next to the 'Library' mural," I said. "Isn't that the one by Bernard Zakheim, the artist who painted the murals in the Medical School building up on Parnassus Street?"

"That's the same guy," Brody replied. "But the one here shows a man taking Marx's *Das Kapital* off the shelf. I never liked that Zakheim. Never trusted him. He seemed shifty like a lot of those Commie Jews."

I noticed Dennis frowning and shaking his head, but I kept a neutral expression.

"Sure enough, he asked if he could paint me in the mural and I agreed, but then he showed me reading a book called *Weird*

Spirit. What a nerve! I heard they wouldn't let him back into Poland in '20 after the war. Doesn't surprise me. Look what Bela Kun and those Commie Jews did to Hungary!"

"Did you serve in the war?" asked Dennis.

"I served my country in four wars," Brody replied. "I was an enlisted man when I fought the Spanish in Cuba in '98, then the Boxer rebels in China, then the Filipinos in '01, but they made me a Lt. Colonel in the Great War. I wanted to go fight the Krauts in France, but they kept me here in charge of coastal artillery. I'm too old for this war, but it's a good thing in some ways."

"What do you mean?" I asked.

"I don't like it at all that Roosevelt hooked us up with Stalin and I have mixed feelings about our fighting Hitler. The Japs, sure. Like Senator Phelan said, they were always going to try to take us over, and we were always going to have to fight to keep this a white man's country."

Brody walked over to a bookshelf and pulled out a large scrapbook. He opened it and took out something folded up. He unfolded it — a poster from Phelan's 1920 campaign: "Keep California White" it read.

Brody turned and spoke directly to Dennis. "If you ask me, Hitler shouldn't have gotten greedy, and he never should have joined up with the Japs. He did some good things — got rid of the Commies and the socialists, put the Jews in their place, gave the people back their pride."

Dennis frowned. "I spent a lot of time traveling around Germany and meeting people. What I saw doesn't really fit with what you are saying. You're not one of those American Firsters still dragging their feet instead of working hard for our V for Victory campaign, are you?"

Brody reddened and took a minute to respond. When he replied he spoke in a clipped but more measured tone of voice. "Young man, I've lived a bit longer than you and I've done my share of seeing the world, too. I could tell you stories of what we had to put up with when we were fighting for our lives against the Cubans in '98 and those underhanded *Insurrectos* in the Philippines in '01. Furthermore…"

"I don't think Detective Sullivan is questioning your patriotism," I intervened, "but let's remember what my grandmother used to say at the table when I was a boy in Castelnuovo d'Asti: never discuss politics and religion in polite company."

I stood up. "We can talk about the war another time; we have some nasty business to attend to right now, do we not?"

I took out my cigarettes and lit up a Lucky Strike. Brody walked over to an end table, picked up an ashtray, and handed it to me.

"Colonel Brody," I said, "I'd like to use your telephone if I may. The coroner is waiting to hear from me so he can send an ambulance to pick up the body."

The colonel pointed out a telephone in a niche in the hallway and I dialed the coroner's direct number at the Hall of Justice. I reminded him that he had to pick a trustworthy driver who would keep quiet about this assignment. He assured me he'd already picked a driver and an assistant who would do the job on the QT.

"Gentlemen," I said, "let's go to the 'Library' mural and get this unpleasant duty over with."

We walked downstairs and headed to the southwest corner. I knew we were getting close to Winthrop, because I started to gag. I pulled the handkerchief from the breast pocket of my suit coat and held it over my nose.

"Maybe we should have come here before lunch after all," Dennis said.

The chief had turned Harlan back over, and the dagger stuck out. He seemed to have shrunk. His body was stiff with rigor mortis. There was bruising on the back of his head and his hands looked as though they had bruises around the knuckles, too. But the knife sticking out of his back was what had especially grabbed my attention.

Holding the handkerchief over my nose with my left hand, I bent over to take a closer look at the dagger.

"Look at this, Dennis," I said. "Do you see the letters imprinted on the leather handle?"

Dennis bent over next to me. "Oh, oh, I don't like the looks of this at all," he replied.

"I don't either," I said. "Colonel, you are a military man. You may also know that SPQR means Senātus Populusque Rōmānus — the Senate and the Roman People. The Roman legions carried SPQR banners when they marched to battle."

"Mussolini plastered SPQR all over his big new fascist buildings," Dennis added. "I saw them when I was traveling in Rome and Milan."

Brody took a closer look. "I don't know this man," he said. "The chief said he is Harlan Winthrop. I've seen his name in the papers. Why would somebody stab him with such a distinctive knife? A big kitchen knife would do the job just as well, and there are so many of them out there that the police could never find the owner. This one is pretty unusual, isn't it?"

"Whoever used this knife had to know what he was doing,"

Dennis said. "He obviously wanted the body to be found with a message, and the message is right on the handle. We've got a fascist murder weapon sticking out of a dead body, right next to that pro-Axis slogan RoBerTo."

"Yes," I replied. "I can't help thinking back to what President Roosevelt said in his press conference after Italy invaded France: 'the hand that held the dagger struck it into the back of its neighbor.'"

"Harlan was the president of the War Bonds for Victory drive in San Francisco," Dennis said. "And we are fighting with Free France and England against Italy. So we are sort of wartime neighbors with our ally, France."

I turned to Dennis. "Are you saying the killer chose Winthrop just to make a point?"

Dennis shrugged. "Perhaps he's trying to send a message: if you oppose the Axis power in this city, you're in mortal danger. Maybe I'm jumping to conclusions, but what if he's a fifth column agent? He could be an Axis sympathizer thumbing his nose at us."

Brody chimed in. "It seems like just the other day that General Mola bragged about his fifth column. How he would eventually conquer Madrid during the civil war in Spain." He chuckled, as though he liked the idea. "He said he had four Army columns advancing on the city and one secret fifth column inside, ready to weaken the defense by sabotaging and killing the defenders.

"I have reservations about our fighting Hitler and the Germans," he continued. "But I sure as hell don't want any Axis fifth column sneaking around here 'sowing discord,' as Mayor Rossi said in his speech last week."

Our conversation was interrupted by the sound of voices

and footsteps coming from the front door area. Two middle-aged men dressed in white uniforms and wearing white surgical masks approached us. One of them carried a rolled-up stretcher.

"I'm Kevin McCarthy and this is George Bonn," said the taller of the two after I introduced myself. "We're from the coroner's office."

Bonn gestured toward the body. "I guess this is the guy who will be riding with us this afternoon," he said in an emotionless voice. "He's marinating pretty good here. The sooner we get him into cold storage the better, right governor? You can come and see him in the morgue; visiting hours are all day long. And don't worry, mum's da woid."

We moved aside as McCarthy and Bonn unrolled their stretcher and lifted Harlan Winthrop from the floor onto the canvass device. "The guy must have bled out somewhere else," McCarthy said. "But you probably didn't need me to tell you that." Without another word they lifted the stretcher and walked away down the hallway toward the front door.

"I wouldn't want their job," I said.

"They must see some terrible things," Dennis said. "You can't really blame them if they try to lighten things up by cracking wise once and a while."

"Yes," Brody agreed. "I just turned twenty when I survived those sneak attacks by the so-called freedom fighters in Catubig and Balangiga back in 1900 and 1901. You wouldn't believe what it was like, so I won't even try to describe it. But I'll tell you, we would've gone stark raving mad if we hadn't been able to kid around and joke about what they did to us, and what we did to them, back then in that Philippine War."

I found myself looking at the part of the mural on the right hand side of the window.

"You know," I said, "he painted this during the Depression, but what a negative message Zakheim left here. The men in the library are reading about a bunch of terrible current events; the headlines show the country going down the drain; one man is reaching for a copy of *Das Kapital,* and another is reading that Red union paper *The Western Worker.*"

"Maybe it's time we painted a more positive mural here to help us survive this war," Brody said.

He walked us to the front door and we said goodbye.

"You can open the tower again as soon as you get rid of that RoBerTo sign." I gave him my business card. "Once you make sure the mural looks like it did before the killer defaced it, call me and I'll notify the two cops at the door that they can go back to their usual work at the Central Station."

"And remember," Dennis added, "no one is to know anything about this."

Chapter 4   Thursday, April 2, 1942

"Tony, come and see this, hurry," Flora called out to me. I got up from my desk and went downstairs, wondering what she was so excited about.

She was standing in front of our large living room window that looks out across the bay and toward Golden Gate Bridge. A huge aircraft carrier with B-25 bombers lashed down on its deck was just about to pass under the bridge and sail into the Pacific. Five other warships followed.

They were a fearsome sight. Their gray-blue camouflage paint contrasted ominously with the clear, vibrant colors of the sky, the bay and the Marin hills in the bright morning light.

"That's the Hornet," I said, "on its way back to the Hawaiian Islands."

"Why don't they just fly out there?"

"They don't carry enough fuel, so they have to go by ship."

"Can they bomb Japan from Hawaii?"

"I don't think so, but maybe they can sail from Pearl Harbor and then bomb them."

"I'd hate to think we were going to bomb any cities in Japan, the way the Nazis did in England."

"I agree, Flora," I said. "I'd better get back to my desk and finish these calls I have to make."

Upstairs, I was about to pick up the telephone when it rang.

"Good morning Tony," said my brother.

"Enzo, how are things in Pescadero? Have any of your parishioners been visited by the Army or the police?"

"My mechanic's brother had his fishing boat impounded. He's a sixty-year-old man!"

"Well I spent the last two days at a meeting with the archbishop about the roundup of Italian aliens and talking on the telephone to anxious *paisans* from here to Benicia and Pacifica."

"We have the same thing going on down here in San Mateo County," Lorenzo said. "A lot of these Italian farmers and fishermen never bothered to learn English, and their wives never even gave it a thought. Now they are lining up at the rectory — 'Father Lorenzo, what should we do? Why are they saying such bad things about us? Are they going to take us away?' Their kids, that's a different story — most of them don't speak any Italian or go to church, for that matter."

"I know, I know," I said. "Yesterday Joe DiMaggio called me. He was frantic. I had to hold the telephone receiver away from my ear! His mom and dad are up there in Pittsburg, but Joe thinks General DeWitt might move them out of their house just to make a point about his policy of 'No Exceptions' to the removal order on the basis of a family's celebrity.

"I told Joe I would ask Archbishop Mitty to call the general and remind him that Giuseppe and Rosalie live outside the prohibited zone. But I also told Joe that nobody could stop DeWitt from prohibiting his dad from managing his restaurant at Fisherman's Wharf, because the restaurant *is* in the prohibited zone. He was so mad he told me 'Tony, I thought I could count on you, but I guess not' and hung up on me."

"We are living in terrible times," Lorenzo said. "This is what happens when people stop praying to Christ our King and start saluting monsters like Hitler and Mussolini. I fear we will have to fight for our lives against a horrible 20th Century form of paganism."

"Enzo, Enzo," I said, "spare me the sermon. You are preaching to the choir here. I still have about a dozen telephone calls to answer before we leave for Pescadero."

"Actually," Lorenzo said, "that's what I called about. You hadn't called and I wanted to make sure you and Flora still plan to drive down here for our Holy Thursday dinner and my Maundy Thursday Mass at St. Anthony's in the evening."

"If you let me get off the telephone and answer my other calls, I'll pack the car and we will get on our way."

He chuckled. "All right, I get the point, Tony. I'm always the long-winded one, not you."

I laughed back. "It's a nice day, Enzo. I want Flora to enjoy the drive, so I plan to take the Great Highway along the Ocean Beach and then go south on Highway 1. Flora loves looking out at the ocean glittering on a sunny day and I enjoy the drive."

"Be sure to allow extra time today," Lorenzo said. "I drove back and forth to the city last Saturday. The trip took twice as long as usual. I think it's because the immigration people opened their detention center."

"I know about that camp in Sharp Park," I said, "it's in that canyon next to the golf course where the city put out of work drifters during the Depression. According to Monday's paper they have almost two hundred people there already. Of course, it takes truckloads of food and bedding and all to maintain it. I heard they are still building it, so lots of construction material and workers will also be going back and forth."

"How long do you think it'll take, Tony?"

"We should be there by 4:00."

I said goodbye, lit my second Lucky Strike of the morning and started returning my calls. A few reassuring words, sometimes in Italian and sometimes in English, did the trick.

But not the call to Franklin Street. The archbishop himself insisted on speaking to me, again, about the DiMaggio family. "Your Excellency," I said, "General DeWitt takes himself so seriously that it's almost impossible to get through to him once he has made up his mind about something."

"Tony," he replied, "do you have any reason to believe that he has a bias against Catholics like so many of our officials?"

"Not that I have experienced," I replied, "and I haven't heard that from any of my legal colleagues, including Mr. Molinari, who helped organize the Citizens Committee to Aid Italians Loyal to the United States."

"I have utmost respect for Mr. Molinari. He'd make an excellent judge."

"Yes, but I think DeWitt is prejudiced against *Italians*. After all, even President Roosevelt is prejudiced and publicly condemns us and contradicts himself. First, he says we're just comic opera singers so we aren't dangerous, and then he repeats the old insult that we're dagger-wielding sneaks."

"I think that's terribly unfair, Tony."

"Yes. My suggestion, Excellency, is that we wait it out and be patient. They're not going to be able to move all the Italians out of California the way they are doing with the Japs. There are too many of us, they can't afford the cost of it, and they need us in the factories and shipyards. Besides, we're white, not Japanese!"

As I was finishing my call to the archbishop, Flora was standing impatiently in the doorway pointing to her wrist watch. She had on a deep blue dress with a cameo pin at the cleavage. The dress looked great with her long dark brown hair, clear olive complexion, and still youthful looking figure. We both regret that God chose to deny us children, but at a moment like this, I thanked Him for Flora. I said a little prayer to St. Priscilla.

I had showered and shaved when I got up, so I hung up my dressing gown and put on a pair of light gray pleated slacks. The freshly laundered white shirt and dark-blue V-neck sweater were folded on the bed, beside a pair of argyle socks. I slipped on my dark brown penny loafers, took my light topcoat out of the closet and started for the front door.

"You look very casual for a Holy Day," Flora remarked, with mischief in her brown eyes. "You also look pretty smart and handsome for a man over fifty."

"One of the reasons I have loved you for so long is that you always tell the truth," I replied with a smile. She tilted her head to the side and laughed as she swatted me on the shoulder with the folded copy of *San Francisco News* she held in her right hand. In her left, she held a basket with two bottles of Nebbiolo.

"Flattery will get you nowhere, counselor," she said. "Let's get on the road."

Sure enough, from the Cliff House to the detention center in Sharp Park, we were part of a slow moving procession of Army vehicles with big white stars on their doors and hoods, painted a dull olive drab. South of Rockaway Beach, though, the traffic was light all the way to Pescadero.

The hills on our left were still a vibrant green from the fall and winter rains, the fields a rich brown awaiting the spring crops to bloom. From Moss Beach to El Granada, to San Gregorio, we drove along the edge of the cliffs high above the beaches with the azure Pacific stretching to the horizon. Flora betrayed her usual anxiety about the precipitous drop right alongside the road. "It's beautiful, Tony, but don't you dare look," she said for the thousandth time.

As we drove into town, the traffic on Pescadero Creek Road and Main Street surprised me. I asked Lorenzo about it after we parked at his rectory by St. Anthony's.

"Fred Durante told me that a bunch of his Portuguese relatives and friends are moving out here," Lorenzo said. "They figure with the war and all, they can buy and plow up a lot of land that has just been sitting there, plant more artichokes, fava beans, and — well, pretty much anything grows here — and they can make good money while helping the country out."

"I thought I saw some Mexicans camping along Pescadero Creek," Flora said. "There was a teenage Mexican girl carrying a little baby walking along the road and three Mexican men wearing dirty old clothes standing outside Michangelo's grocery store on Main Street."

Flora started unpacking her carryall.

"Maybe you haven't seen them, but there've been Mexicans coming to San Mateo County since they had their revolution," I said.

Lorenzo agreed. "There were a few around the time I married you two at St. Anthony's."

"That was in 1915," Flora said. "I don't recall any Mexicans then."

"Well, back then, most of my parishioners were Italian and

Portuguese," Lorenzo explained. "The Mexicans were mostly up around Half Moon Bay. They went to Our Lady of the Pillar. But that atheistic socialist president, Plutarco Calles, made things so hard for Catholics that they had that Cristeros rebellion down there. Thousands of them left the country. Several families moved into our area. Tony, you're the scholar in the family — when was that, about ten years ago?"

"Longer ago than that," I answered. "I think that was in '25, and I'd say it was more like tens of thousands of Catholics, at least, had to leave for fear of their lives. Flora, maybe you remember how upset I was for days after that Knights of Columbus meeting when I learned that Calles executed Father Miguel Pro — shot him without a trial."

"You know," Lorenzo said, "most Mexicans have a hard life. We should show them Christian charity, not blame them for being poor."

"I'm not being mean," Flora said. "It's just upsetting to see them. I don't know. They make me nervous. Of course we should be charitable to them, but why do they look so angry? They just scare me."

Lorenzo sighed. "One of my parishioners, a man by the name of Gilberto Perez, told me this: 'We Mexicans have a cross to bear, Father Lorenzo; we are so far away from God but so close to the United States'.

"I can understand he might think God has abandoned his children in Mexico, with its terrible treatment of the faithful. But I asked him what he meant about it being hard to be close to our country; after all he came here for a better life. He can make enough money to raise his family here, and worship freely. He told me it's our fault that Mexico is so poor — we take its oil and minerals and the money goes to their politicians and not to the people."

"That's the socialist line," I replied. "I hope you corrected him. After all, if it hadn't been for President Coolidge and Dwight Morrow, and of course Pius XI, they would still have a civil war going on down there between the Cristeros and the Calles government."

"I haven't seen Mr. Perez for a while," Lorenzo said, "he seems to have stopped going to Mass. But the next time I see him, I will remind him that our government will start a new program in September — bringing Mexicans to work in our fields. They'll make a lot more money than they could in Mexico. So, to me, it's a good thing that they are close to the USA."

"That seems like a good thing to me, too," Flora said. "But I'm getting a headache from all of this political talk. Or maybe I'm just hungry. I'm going in to help Maria with the dinner. It's almost five o'clock."

"Tony," said Lorenzo, "speaking of Mexicans I wanted to talk with you about something that's been on my mind. Maybe we can discuss it during our walk on the beach tomorrow."

"Of course," I replied, "and coincidentally I would like to tell *you* something related to Palm Sunday as well."

We walked through the back door of the rectory and washed our hands at the sink in the laundry room when Flora announced that dinner was ready. Maria, Lorenzo's housekeeper and cook, joined us as always. The table was crowded with a large bowl of polenta, a platter of lamb chops over which Maria had sprinkled freshly picked mint and oregano leaves, a bowl of spinach sautéed in garlic and onions, and a round loaf of bread made without salt.

After Lorenzo led us in saying grace, I opened one of the bottles of Nebbiolo, poured us each a glass and raised mine in a toast: "To Christ our King! Let's do justice to this food and drink."

Chapter 5   Friday, April 3, 1942

Lorenzo and I walked the two blocks to St. Anthony's. "This church needs a new coat of paint," I said.

"I know, I know," he replied. "All through the Depression I didn't ask the archbishop to paint it because I knew there was no money. Now he says he can't afford it because of the war. I reminded him that our poor little church is seventy-three years old now and built of wood. Doesn't it make sense to keep some money back from parishes with grand churches like Saint Boniface and Saint Agnes and paint our humble place of worship?"

I nodded. "He tends to give in to those well-heeled San Francisco Catholics who pressure him and donate big sums to the Church. It's not fair, I agree."

Only a handful of worshippers joined us at the eight o'clock Mass, most of them older ladies who could have been either Portuguese or Italian. Only two men were there and they were accompanying their wives. Since almost all of the twenty pews in the tiny church were empty, it was hard to miss anyone. I didn't notice anyone who looked Mexican.

After Mass we drove the two miles to the ocean, parking next to the short path to the beach. We rolled up our trousers, took off our shoes and socks and locked them in the car.

We walked down to the water's edge where the sand was firm and the walking more pleasant. The morning was clear again, with a chilly wind that felt fresh and invigorating.

"So," I said, "we both wanted to talk about something. Who should go first?"

He gave me a playful punch on my shoulder. "Why don't you go first? I'm your older brother and I'm more patient than you are."

"First, you have to promise me you will keep what I have to tell you secret," I said. "It could very well be something that affects our national defense. I haven't even told Flora about this yet, but I'm going to tell her and I'm going to tell you because I need your advice."

I told him the whole story — the murder, the dagger with the letters SPQR on the handle, the RoBerTo sign painted on the mural, Chief O'Reilly asking me to work with Sullivan on the case, and the importance of secrecy.

I explained to him that Sullivan and I didn't want to jump to conclusions, but that we had a theory: somebody or some group killed Winthrop because he headed the war bonds drive and they hoped to scare the public about a fifth column operating in San Francisco.

Lorenzo remained silent while I told him the story. The waves made a swishing sound as they washed up onto the beach, the cold water sloshing over my bare feet. Up ahead, a high bluff jutted out into the ocean as the waves crashed on the rocks below.

"I'm getting a chill down my spine," Lorenzo finally said. "Recently one of my parishioners told me about a secret society here in the Bay Area. He said it's a small group, but they want to find a way to show that they oppose this war. It was this man's son who first came to me. He is very upset because his dad won't let him enlist in the Army at seventeen."

"Where did he get his information?"

"I don't know if what he told me is true or not," Lorenzo replied. "I don't know what to think. I thought you would know what to do with this information. You're the head of one of the draft boards. Now you are telling me you think some fifth column is really operating here?"

We came to the end of the beach, where the massive rocks at the bottom of the bluff blocked our way. "It's time to walk back," I said. "Let's drive back to town. You can tell me all about it over breakfast."

Chapter 6 Friday, April 3, 1942

e parked in front of Durante's Tavern. Fred had put up snappy new Venetian Blinds in the front windows. The latest model Neon sign, advertising Spreckels Ice Cream, was glowing red in the morning light.

"Business must be good," I said to Lorenzo.

We greeted a clutch of sleepy looking young men in wrinkled Army uniforms standing in front, their caps and hats pushed back and tilted to one side in the latest off-duty style.

"Good morning, Father," said Fred Durante with a big smile on his moon-shaped face, as we joined a line of people waiting to be seated. He turned his attention to me. "Counselor," he added, "down here for your Holy Week tradition, are you? I figured you boys would show up about this time, so I reserved your favorite table over in the corner where you will have a little more privacy."

Everyone nodded and smiled. A few of the older ladies gave Lorenzo little bows as we walked to our table. Fred came over with a pot of coffee and filled our cups. "Your regular?" he asked. "Pancakes and bacon and eggs for you," he said, looking at me, "and an omelet with garlic, onions, and mushrooms for you, Father?" We thanked him and he hurried off to the kitchen with our order.

"All right, let me explain," Lorenzo began. "I can't tell you the whole story because that would break the seal of the confessional, but it all started when the son of one of my most devout and active parishioners, Pedro Quintana, came to me the day after Pearl Harbor. The son's name is Peter; he's seventeen years old. He will finish high school in May. He wants to enlist the day after graduation. Since he's only seventeen, he needs his parents to sign off. His dad told him he would never give his approval."

"Why not?" I asked. "I have spoken with a number of fathers who consulted with me about the procedure for giving approval for this. None of them have wanted to say no. They are all worried about their boys, sure, but they understand that their sons want to do their duty. I tell them that this is a war against a monstrous evil pagan foe and to always remember we are fighting for *God* as well as our country.

"You said this Pedro Quintana is a devout Catholic so I would think he would have no trouble understanding this."

"That's just what I asked Peter," Lorenzo replied. "So I suggested to Peter that he sit down with his father and ask him to explain why he doesn't want to approve of his enlisting. He came back a few days later — I remember it well because the paper that day had a big headline about Italy declaring war on us — and Peter said his dad refused to talk about it. He wouldn't approve and that was that.

"So I told Peter that I would come to the Quintana house and talk to him and his parents. They live on a farm outside of town. I called Pedro. First, he refused to discuss it. Then he said, 'All right, Father, come to dinner and I will explain.'"

Fred returned with our breakfasts, and we tucked into our pancakes and omelet. "Boys," he said, "you look like you have a lot to talk about. I'll just leave this pot of coffee here for you." We thanked him and Lorenzo continued his story.

"We had a nice dinner, and then we all sat down in the living room, Pedro, his wife Manuela, and Peter. There was a scrapbook on the table next to the sofa. Peter asked his father about it and Pedro admitted he'd kept it well hidden. 'I'm going to tell you and Father Bosco a story,' he said, 'a true story, so please, don't interrupt me until I finish.' What he told me was shocking.

"He opened the scrapbook and showed us photos and newspaper clippings from Mexican newspapers, going all the way back to the middle of the twenties. The first photographs were of Pedro and Manuela getting married in 1923. And there were pictures of little baby Peter, who was born in 1925. But most of the photos showed Pedro — Pedro on a horse holding a rifle, Pedro in a group of men wearing sombreros with bandoliers crossed over their chests and pistols strapped to their waists, Pedro with General Enrique Gorostieta!

"Tony, Pedro was part of the League for Religious Freedom, the Cristeros! He was one of the leaders in the war against the government of Plutarco Calles! The government that oppressed Catholics in Mexico and murdered priests!

"Peter and I were flabbergasted! Pedro had always seemed very devout, but he was quiet and shy — not at all a person I would imagine as a rebel fighter."

"I met a number of League members back when the Cristero war was raging down in Mexico," I said. "That was when I went up and down California with four of my Knights of Columbus brothers giving speeches to raise money for The Million Dollar Fund. The money went for the K of C campaign to end the war and help all the refugees fleeing Mexico. Each and every League fighter I met was well educated, articulate, and well-mannered — the idea that the Cristeros were just a bunch of bloodthirsty bandits was, like we said at the time, 'A Big Lie.'"

"I understand," Lorenzo said. "Pedro told me that he was so worried about Manuela and Peter, he sent them to California, far away from the fighting. He has relatives here in San Mateo County. He sent them enough money so they could help her buy a farm big enough to support them while he kept fighting.

"Manuela managed the farm until Pedro joined them. After General Gorostieta was killed in battle and the rebels gave up he refused to continue to live in Mexico. Peter was four years old then. Because he came here when he was two, his only memories of his dad are from when Pedro came to Pescadero in 1929."

"This reminds me of a lot of the families in North Beach," I said. "I'd bet that Peter, like a lot of children of immigrants, especially when their parents deliberately don't talk about their lives before they came here, don't even speak very good Spanish."

"He doesn't speak Spanish at all!" Lorenzo replied. "He told me he wishes his mom and dad didn't have such strong accents — it's embarrassing to him. The first thing he said after his dad told the story about fighting with the Cristeros was 'Why didn't you ever tell me about any of this? Why did you both hide all of this from me? And what does this have to do with not approving me to fight for our country?

"'You fought for what you believed in, the freedom to be a good Catholic. All right, I understand.

"'I want to fight for what *I* believe in!

"'I'm American, not Mexican!' Peter said. 'I want to fight for the *Four* Freedoms President Roosevelt talks about — freedom of worship, freedom of speech, freedom from fear, and freedom from want. Hitler, Mussolini and the Emperor of Japan, they want to take away all our freedoms.'

"Pedro was stony faced. He hadn't moved since Peter started ranting.

"Then Peter called his father a hypocrite! He was pacing the room. He said, 'You sit here and brag about fighting for religious freedom when you were young but you won't let me do the same thing?'"

"Peter's point of view is understandable," I said. "I'm surprised his father is so unsympathetic."

"And Tony, Manuela had been sitting quietly wringing her hands while Pedro told the whole story. But after Peter's outburst she looked down at her hands and said, 'Peter, your dad and I care about your safety. We don't want you to get hurt in a war. But we also don't want you to fight in *this* war — and we believe that very deeply.'"

I nodded. "The Cristeros I met almost twenty years ago were zealots — all of them. I imagine that Pedro loves his son and wants him to be safe. He and Manuela may *also* feel that our country does not respect the cause the Cristeros fought and died for — a constitution with Catholic values written into it, like the one in Ireland! Our constitution supports separation of church and state, but Pedro and Manuela may disagree with that."

"I see what you mean," Lorenzo said. "They didn't have to think about this while Peter was growing up. They could be devout Catholics here in Pescadero and not think about their lives back in Mexico or about our whole setup here in America. But I can see how they might feel they have to take a stand against Peter possibly dying for a country with 'a wall of separation between church and state.' They might feel they would be sacrificing their boy to an alien principle."

"Also," I continued, "think about this: their fellow 'freedom fighters' in Mexico hated and despised socialism, even the kind of mixed up version in the Calles regime, but now President Roosevelt is an ally fighting with Josef Stalin, head of the biggest socialist type government in the world!"

"That would explain the secret society Pedro told me and Peter about that night," Lorenzo said. "Pedro and a number of his friends — veterans of the Cristero rebellion who live in the Bay Area — they organized something called The Clermont Society. They named it after the city in France where Pope Urban II called for the First Crusade. It started out as just a social group, where they got together once a month, drank tequila, talked about Mexican politics and told stories about the good old days when they were shouting *Viva Cristo Rey* and fighting the *Federales*."

Lorenzo poured us the rest of the coffee.

"Enzo, I don't know if you realize this, but you're pretty much telling me everything. What about the seal of the confessional?"

"I guess you're right, Tony, but sometimes we have to be flexible about our vows if our country is in danger.

"And there's a political angle, too: Pedro told me that they never forgave the US for not supporting the Cristeros side in the rebellion. And last October, when Roosevelt began sending military aid to Russia, they decided they had to do something to show their opposition to our helping out the world's most powerful atheistic communist nation."

By this time, Fred's wife had cleared away our dishes. Now she asked if we wanted any more coffee. I accepted her offer. "This coffee is so good, I'd love some more. Thanks."

I stirred some cream into my coffee and reflected for a minute or two. Lorenzo was looking concerned.

"Did Pedro say anything explicitly about creating a fifth column?" I asked. "Maybe 'doing something' just means writing letters to President Roosevelt, or to the editor of the four papers in the city. What exactly did he say?"

"No, Tony, he didn't say anything that dramatic, but I got the impression he was very serious and he never agreed, while I was there, to approve Peter's enlistment. According to Peter after last Sunday's Palm Sunday Mass, he still hasn't changed his mind."

"I can't do anything about this today," I said. "I'll be in church with you for the Good Friday service this afternoon. But after we drive home this evening, I need to call Detective Sullivan. We may need to come back down here to talk with Pedro Quintana."

Chapter 7   Monday, April 6, 1942

Buses were lined up on Fell Street and Oak Street as I drove across the panhandle of Golden Gate Park on Masonic Avenue. Dennis was standing in front of St. Agnes Church, hatless, waiting for me to pick him up for our trip down the coast to Pescadero.

He was wearing a shoulder holster for his revolver. There was a bulge on the left side of his brown leather jacket.

On the phone I'd mentioned I wouldn't be wearing a suit and tie today, just a sport coat and slacks, and that he should wear something comfortable for the long drive. I guess he took me literally.

"There's no point in our going down to the Hall of Justice first," I'd told him during our phone call yesterday. "The whole area between Pacific Heights and downtown will be jammed up because the Army will be moving the Japs out of the city by the busload. Flora and I saw the buses already lined up, dozens of them, when we came back to the city from Pescadero on Saturday."

Dennis walked over to the car as I pulled up to the church. "Good morning, Tony," he said, "I hope you and your family had a good Easter."

"As good as it could be," I replied, "considering all that happened. I'm still going over it all in my mind."

Dennis settled into the passenger seat. "One thing I wondered," he said, "is how will we get this Quintana guy to talk to us about his organization? You told me the Clermont Society is secret, so what do we do if he refuses to tell us anything? You don't have any official position, and my badge doesn't give me any authority in San Mateo County."

"That's a good point," I answered. "And there's more you need to know.

"Chief O'Reilly sent a telegram to the FBI asking if they had any information about Pedro Quintana after I talked to him about all of this on Saturday. It turns out Quintana was one of the men arrested back in 1927 down near Tucson, Arizona, for trying to smuggle guns across the border to Mexico to help in the Cristero rebellion."

"So he has a prison record?"

"No, here's what happened. The Border Patrol got a tip that Pedro was part of a gang that put together a truckload of eight boxes of Winchester and Mauser rifles and ammunition. They located the truck before the guys left. They arrested Pedro and three other guys in Sierra Vista, but they didn't have enough evidence to charge Pedro. The leader of the gang was Pedro's friend José Gándara.

"They convicted Gándara, but the Knights of Columbus and a bunch of bishops, including our Archbishop Hanna, talked President Hoover into pardoning him back in 1930.

"The chief and I decided we needed to have a deputy sheriff with us when we went to see Quintana. He will be waiting for us in Pescadero."

As I expected, the traffic was much worse between the city and the Sharp Park Camp today. Buses filled with Japanese families, driving caravan style, jammed the Skyline and the Coast Highway. With all of the stopping and starting, I had to do so much gear shifting and braking that I was getting tired by the time we got to Rockaway Beach.

"Tony," said Dennis, "you are looking a bit weary. Would you like me to take the wheel? I've never gotten to drive a Buick before, and I'm a good driver. I'm not afraid of driving high up on the side of a mountain. It would be nothing compared to driving from Turin to Nuremberg and then back to Bologna and Rome when I was traveling in Italy and Germany."

"Nobody but me has ever driven my Century," I said. "I'm kind of protective of it. But I know that route from Torino to Germany. If you could do that, this forty or so miles should be easy."

Stopping for gas in Montara, we bought two chicken sandwiches and two Cokes at the grocery store next to the Flying A station. We sat down at one of the picnic benches in the little garden next to the grocery store. "How is it you had a car in Europe?" I asked. "Everybody I know travels around by train."

Dennis smiled. "I'm kind of embarrassed to say so, but my dad gave me a car for a graduation present. In England and Ireland, I did all my traveling on trains and buses. Then I took a ferry from Dover to Calais and then a train to Paris, where my car was waiting for me — a shiny black two door Citroen 7CV. I drove all over France, down to Italy, all around in Italy and then up to Germany. I went as far as Budapest and Prague. It was a great opportunity — I learned a lot."

"You mentioned Torino," I said. "Did you visit Castelnuovo d'Asti, my home town?"

"No," Dennis replied. "After a few days in Turin my friend and I wanted to visit all of the villas designed by the architect Palladio that Professor Hennessy told us about at St. Mary's. So we went to the Veneto and didn't really explore the Piedmont. So, you were born over there?"

"That's right," I said. "I came to San Francisco when I was

eleven years old. My brother Enzo, Lorenzo, who you will meet today, came before me, and two younger brothers and my sister came over after me. One of those younger brothers went back after the Pope signed the Lateran Treaty in '29. He is a priest in Torino. Mussolini put him in prison for two years because he was the spiritual advisor for a Catholic Action young people's club. The Black Shirts closed down all those clubs. When Alfredo and his young men and women protested, Mussolini threw them all into prison. He's okay now but he'll never be the same. When I saw him on my last visit four years ago, he was like a ghost of his former self."

"That's terrible, Tony," Dennis said. "Can you keep in touch with him now that Italy declared war on us?"

"I wrote to him in December after that happened, but I haven't heard anything back. I hope he will be safe, but I know that anything could happen, so he is especially in our prayers these days."

"That's a terrible story. I'm so sorry," Dennis said.

"My parents are dead. My brothers and sister and I own the house in Castelnuovo d'Asti. One of my cousins lives there now. I don't know if I'll ever see it again, what with this war, but I hope so."

I got up, threw our Coke bottles and sandwich papers into the trash can, and handed Dennis the keys to my Century. "All right," I said, "I feel much better. Now let's see what you can do with a *real* car!"

For the first ten minutes, I had to force myself not to tell Dennis he was driving too close to the edge of the highway. I'm clearly not used to seeing the world from the passenger seat. But he handled my Century like he was born to the job. I began to enjoy the view, and we rode into Pescadero right on schedule.

Lorenzo and a gangly man in his sixties wearing a deputy's uniform that looked too tight were waiting for us at a table in Durante's. We introduced ourselves and shook hands.

"Good morning, Commissioner Bosco, my name is Deputy Arnaldo Gonsalves," he said. "I know what yur thinkin: what's a old man like you doin in that uniform?"

"You're a poor mind reader, deputy," I replied. "I'm not a detective like Dennis here, but it's obvious that since you retired, you've been enjoying your wife's cooking more than you should. Or maybe your uniform shrank in the closet. And now the youngsters have all left to do their duty, and Sheriff Carmody has sort of 'cancelled your leave', am I right?"

"I knew it when I saw you came in the door," Gonsalves said, pointing at me, "here comes a couple of smart big city boys. Well, so far you ain't disappointed me."

He gave out a loud series of goodhearted laughs.

"I can see we're all going to get along just fine," Dennis said. He took off his leather jacket and draped it over the back of his chair. The handle of his revolver stuck out of his shoulder holster.

"Looks like you've got the Colt .38 Police Special with a five-inch barrel, Detective," Gonsalves said. "I don't think you'll need it down here. All the bad guys are up in Frisco, ain't that right, Father Lorenzo?"

"Well, if that's so," Dennis replied, "what's that .45 that you're wearing, pray tell? Is it just in case some of those Frisco hoods decide to move down south?"

Gonsalves chuckled. "My .45 went to France with me back in 1918. I would only be halfway dressed if I left it at home."

"We're glad that you got fully dressed to come to work," I said, "so let's have Fred bring us a pot of coffee and get down to business.

"I don't know how much Enzo told you about why we need to interview Pedro Quintana. Chief O'Reilly asked Sheriff Carmody to help us out with a special assignment."

"What's it all about, Commissioner?"

"We can't let you in on all the details — it's a defense matter. We need your San Mateo badge to back us up in case Pedro Quintana doesn't want to cooperate. All I can say is that it's important and there's no time to lose. I don't think you'll need your .45 though, just your being there will probably do the trick."

"I know Quintana," Gonsalves said, "he's been here since '29. I don't have no trouble remembering that time. A lot of Mexicans moved here then. The Estrada, Madera, and the Diaz families moved in here at the end of that summer.

"There was a bunch of them, remember, Father? It seemed like our little church just filled up all of a sudden right around when school started."

"That's right, Arnaldo," Enzo said. "The Quintanas had just their one boy, Peter. But the Maderas, the Estradas, and the Diazes, they each had seven or eight children. They are all good Catholics. I've blessed them as they took their first communions and their confirmations. They and the Quintanas attend Mass regularly, well except for the teenagers now. The ladies and their girls help decorate the church at Christmas and Easter time."

"We never had no trouble with Pedro," Arnaldo said, "he's a hard worker and keeps that farm lookin good. His boy works in the grocery store after school.

"Now — them Mexicans camped out along the creek, that's a different story. They're shifty lookin characters, the kids just run wild, and they're all livin like animals out there. I say we should run 'em out of Pescadero, but the Sheriff says they ain't hurtin nobody and they've got no place else to go."

"We all have a duty as Christians to help out the poor," I said.

"Yeah, I know," Arnaldo said, bristling at my reprimand, "but we have a duty to keep our town clean and safe. Them Mexicans along the creek are makin the place dirty. And folks don't like how they stand around on Main Street askin for money. I also get complaints from the ladies. They don't like the way they get stared at by them tough lookin Mexicans who just stand around smoking cigarettes and doin nothing all afternoon."

"I think what Tony is saying is that we have to be extra kind to these folks," Lorenzo said. "Arnaldo, when your people came over here from the Azores, they brought enough money to buy land. They had relatives in San Mateo County who helped them out. Your mom and dad weren't wealthy. They had to work for everything they ever got. But they knew how to read and write.

"The folks in that camp, they come from a whole different and much poorer background. You need to go easy on them."

"Gentlemen," I said, "we can debate about our Christian responsibility for the poor some other time. Right now, we need to get down to the business at hand, as we lawyers like to say.

"Lorenzo, you ride with me and Dennis to the Quintana farm. Deputy, you follow in your car. When we get there, the four of us will ask to see Mr. Quintana, but Deputy, I'd like you to wait outside while we talk to Pedro. National Security, okay?"

Gonsalves shrugged. "Sure, Commissioner, I don't have no problem with that. You're the commanding officer here."

"I hope we can interview him without any difficulty in his home," I added, "but if he refuses we can tell him that Deputy Gonsalves is empowered to take him to the county jail and we can talk there. Hopefully we won't need to do that."

We pulled into the Quintana place and parked next to a 1939 Deluxe Ford, a four-door sedan model with the chrome V8 symbol on its trunk. It was painted black, but the wheels were coated with dried adobe-colored mud. The whole car was grimy and dusty. It looked like somebody had driven out in a country area in the rain, then let the car dry in the sun.

Parked next to the sedan was a well-cared for dark green Ford Model B pickup that was at least ten years old. It was in good condition for a farmer's vehicle. The bed was scratched up but somebody had recently swept it clean.

I knocked on the front door and heard someone walking toward it. The door opened and a prim light-skinned friendly-looking woman wearing an apron over a cotton dress looked at us with surprise.

"Father Lorenzo," she exclaimed, "good morning. I did not expect you."

"Mrs. Quintana," Lorenzo said, "we've come to speak with your husband. This is my brother Tony and his partner Dennis Sullivan. They're from San Francisco. And you know Deputy Gonsalves."

The color had drained from her face. She bunched up the apron in her two hands. "Oh, Father," she said. "I hope this is not about Peter! I thought we explained to you about all that already."

"Mrs. Quintana, it's not about your son, and there's nothing wrong," I assured her. "We just need to talk to your husband. He may be able to help us with something that happened in the city. He's not in trouble, and it shouldn't take long. May we come in, please? The deputy will stay outside."

She opened the door and led us into a living room that looked like it was only used during holidays and special occasions. As she invited us to sit down, Pedro, wearing blue coveralls that had seen hundreds of washings, walked into the room. I was surprised — he was nothing like I had expected.

Instead of the stocky, overweight, Mexican *paisano* I'd seen in countless newsreels, Pedro looked like a college professor dressed for a costume party in a mechanic's coveralls. He reminded me of the Cristero representatives I met during the K of C fundraising campaign. An athletic looking man about my age and height, Pedro had alert, intelligent eyes and an angular clean shaven face. His neatly combed brown thinning hair was parted on the right, and he was wearing rimless bifocal eyeglasses.

"Good morning, Father Lorenzo," he said, "and who are these two gentlemen I have the pleasure to welcome to our home?"

Enzo introduced us and we shook hands. Pedro's hand was that of a banker or lawyer, not a farm worker. He remained standing while I explained the reason for our visit.

"So you're not here to revisit my alleged role in the Gándara rebellion. That, as you might imagine, is a relief. He was pardoned twelve years ago, after all, and I was never charged for a crime."

He smiled a cold smile and said, "What with the war, and all, one never knows what lengths the government is going to go to — how do you put it, Detective — 'protect and serve' the citizens?"

"Mr. Quintana," I said in my best courtroom voice, "we are not here to stir the embers of some long dead fire, to cause you or your family any discomfort about an unpleasant experience you had with the law years ago. The reason for our visit has to do with our national security.

"We want you to tell us about your Clermont Society — what is its purpose and what kinds of activities does it engage in? We are especially interested in your whereabouts on Palm Sunday and the day before Palm Sunday, March 28."

Pedro's eyes widened. He laughed with genuine surprise. "My whereabouts? And our Clermont Society? Well, first of all, who wants to know? You are from the city, correct? You have no jurisdiction here in Pescadero, so why should I answer any questions from you?"

"I was hoping you would be more cooperative," I said. "If you would rather talk to us at the county jail, I will call Deputy Gonsalves, who is waiting on your porch, and he will be happy to conduct you to that facility."

"Gonsalves?" Pedro asked. "That relic? That bigoted ignoramus? I thought he retired years ago. God is my witness it was about time!"

"He has come back to work to serve his country," I replied, "and we're not here to discuss Gonsalves but to interview you. If you have nothing to hide, why don't you simply answer our questions and we will be done with it."

Pedro sighed and sat down. "Commissioner Bosco, I presume you have heard of the Knights of Columbus?"

"Yes," I replied. "Don't patronize me, Mr. Quintana. I am a long-time member. In fact, I was one of the speakers who raised funds for The Million Dollar campaign to assist refugees from the Cristeros War."

"Good for you, Commissioner," Pedro said, "I along with my many brothers salute you for your efforts. We actually got the idea for our Clermont Society from the Knights. We are a small group of veterans from the League for Religious Freedom who live here in San Mateo County. We all belong to the K of C, but they always conduct business in English. We wanted to have a place where we could speak Spanish.

"We get together to socialize and talk about politics, raise money to help out widows of our martyred brothers, and keep alive the cause so many of us died for. We also write letters to politicians, just like the K of C and the bishops did — so successfully that our leader Senor Gándara received his pardon."

"That all sounds quite positive," I said. "And what is your position on the war? According to my brother, you refuse to approve your son to enlist. Does that mean your group opposes the war?"

Pedro stood up and walked to a cabinet by the window. He opened a drawer and took out a cigar. After clipping off the end, he lit up, took a drag and blew out the smoke. He remained standing and looked me in the eye.

"We are very torn by this war," Pedro said, frowning. "Of course we condemn Hitler and Mussolini. The sneak attack on Pearl Harbor can never be approved by any right-thinking American. But we also hate Communism. We worry that by allying with Stalin and his Soviet Union, America will be helping to keep Atheistic Socialism alive!

"I'm too old to fight against the Axis, but if I was drafted I would willingly put my life on the line for our country. I'm an American citizen now, after all. But you can't ask me to give my permission for my son to sign up at seventeen for a war that I'm feeling so divided about.

"When he's eighteen, he can make his own decision, but since I have a say in what he does now, when he's still a boy, I would be a hypocrite if I allowed him to enlist."

"All of this makes sense," Dennis said. "If your organization is no more subversive than the Knights of Columbus, that is as the English say 'jolly good.' But we still need to know where you were on Palm Sunday, and the day before Palm Sunday."

He turned to my brother. "Father Lorenzo," he continued, "was Mr. Quintana at Mass on Palm Sunday?"

"I'm sorry to say, he was not at Mass that day," Enzo admitted. "Mrs. Quintana and Peter were both there, but not Pedro."

"There is no mystery about my whereabouts, Detective," Pedro said. "I was 1100 miles away in El Paso, Texas!"

"Can anyone attest to that?" I asked.

Quintana smirked. "Of course. My neighbors and fellow society members can all confirm my 'alibi' as you police would put it. Jesús Madera, Miguel Estrada, and José Luis Diaz were there with me along with several hundred other people at our annual Palm Sunday outdoor mass at Mount Cristo Rey outside of El Paso.

"The four of us have been making this pilgrimage on Palm Sunday since the cross on top of the mountain was dedicated on the Feast of Christ the King two years ago. My car is still dirty from the trip. I was about to go out and wash it when you showed up. That's why I'm wearing these coveralls. You don't think I go around all the time looking like a *campesino,* do you?"

He waved me away. "Now if that is all, I'd like to get back to my chore," he said. "What is this all about anyway? I'd imagine if there were really some national security issue, the FBI would be here and not the San Francisco Police Department."

"We're not at liberty to tell you that, Mr. Quintana," I replied. "Suffice it to say it's important enough for us to drive almost fifty miles to speak with you. If you don't have any other questions we will be on our way. We thank you on behalf of Chief O'Reilly and wish you a good day."

Chapter 8   Tuesday, April 7, 1942

ennis and I walked into Chief O'Reilly's office just after eight o'clock. He was sitting behind his desk without his uniform jacket, his shirtsleeves rolled up to his elbows. You could see his famous tattoos on his muscular forearms — an anchor and the word "Frisco" on his left arm and the Blessed Virgin Mary on his right.

Dennis was surprised. He obviously didn't know that, after he graduated from Sacred Heart High School, "Big Gerry" worked on sailing ships all over the Pacific for ten years. He even learned to speak Tagalog and still liked to walk three blocks up to Manilatown for a beer and a game or two at the pool room in the Filipino hotel.

"Sit down, boys," he growled, his piercing blue eyes flashing, "and please explain this headline to me."

Two newspapers were lying on the top of his desk. Large banner headlines blared out of the paper on top "JAP VICTORY CONTINUES IN BATAAN. US FORCES IN FULL RETREAT."

He picked up the other newspaper, unfolded it and held up the front page for me and Dennis to see.

"Isn't this the Italian paper?" Dennis asked. "I don't read Italian without a dictionary."

"This is Eddie Sarno's socialist paper," I answered. I looked at the Chief. "I didn't know you could read Italian. I'm impressed."

"I don't read Italian," he snapped. "The press officer downstairs gave this to me and told me what it said. I thought I gave you two strict orders to keep your investigation quiet. How did

Sarno find out about it?"

I took the paper from him and looked at the front page more closely. "Chief," I said, "nobody reads Eddie's paper except a couple dozen or so broken down old men and women trying to relive their younger days when they marched down Columbus Avenue with Anarchist black flags."

I turned to Dennis. "It says here that Attorney Bosco has been seen with a police detective, proving once again that the entire city government is corrupt. From the mayor to the police chief, they're in league with Fascist Bosco's puppet masters. The black dress wearing Catholic so-called men are in lock step with the troglodyte tyrants marching through the world."

I chuckled. "Oh, this is the best part, listen to this: Bosco as usual stinks up the community *'come il puzzo di ammonica al vecchio vespaisiano'* which means like the smell of ammonia in an old toilet."

I turned to the Chief. "There's nothing here that suggests that Eddie Sarno knows about our investigation. We saw him and his Commie pals Richmond and Quinn on Broadway the other day. We don't need to take him seriously, Chief."

"I wish I could be as nonchalant about this as you seem to be," O'Reilly said. "We can't afford this kind of publicity at all!

"Yesterday, this photographer woman — some kind of Red, I bet — was down in Japantown taking pictures of the Japs lining up to get on the buses. The lieutenant down there telephoned me from the call box near the Raphael Weill School, all upset because she was refusing to move out of the way so the officers could keep things orderly.

"I finally went down there and tried to talk some sense into her head. All she would do was give me the old familiar line about how the Japs have this right and that right and how she had the right to take their pictures."

"I hope you didn't arrest her," I said. "You would just be making a martyr out of her. Nobody will ever see those pictures anyway except a bunch of Reds who read things like *The People's World*."

"No, I just asked her to cooperate with the officers," said the chief. "They are just trying to make things easy for the Japs. She didn't like it when I told her to remember that they bombed us, not the other way around."

"Chief," Dennis said, "you might think I'm too green to say anything here, but when I was in Germany and Italy I saw how hard it is to talk sense to those Commies and fascists who are true believers.

"And they are experts in using propaganda — photographs, even movies. Maybe the best thing would be to confiscate her film. That way it could never be used against us in the Red newspaper."

"That's a good point, Dennis," the chief said, "if the government had cracked down harder on Hitler, before he got into the government, maybe he wouldn't be making war on the whole civilized world now."

"Speaking of propaganda," Dennis said, "I've been thinking more about Harlan Winthrop's murderer. We don't have any reason to thinks it's anybody connected to this anti-Russian Clermont Society, which isn't a fifth column outfit anyway. But what if somebody wants us to *think* that the murderer had a pro-Axis motive — killing Winthrop and then painting RoBerTo on the wall by his body?"

"You mean somebody from the Commie side," asked the chief, "like Eddie Sarno and his Red pals? It's true, they've been making these attacks on Tony, the mayor and myself for a long time, but why would they go so far as to kill somebody? And why now?"

"I can think of two reasons," I said. "One is that the roundup of the Japs is a perfect opportunity to make the police and the mayor's office look bad.

"The Reds have been making this 'bleeding heart' line for a long time — you know the rhetoric: how the bad American Capitalist Imperialists exploit 'the people.' Especially poor folks. Especially the downtrodden Colored people. Remember those black boys that the Commie lawyers defended down there in Alabama?"

"They called them the Scottsboro Boys, didn't they?" Dennis said.

"That's right. The other reason the Reds could actually be behind this is that they've always hated Harlan Winthrop, all the way back to the big strike in '34."

I didn't want to seem like a know it all, but Dennis seemed to need a history lesson. "Look, back then Harlan was trying to kick the Red leader of the dockworkers, Barry Rhodes, out of the country.

"That young editor of the *San Francisco Chronicle* even told me he went to a meeting with Winthrop, the other shipping company owners and a bunch of bankers. They were talking about hiring a gunman to assassinate Rhodes. And Rhodes is back on trial now because the government is trying to deport him back to England again."

"So the Commies hated Winthrop's guts because he wanted to eliminate Rhodes," the chief said. "And I wouldn't put it past them to kill Winthrop and then try to throw the blame on the

Mussolini lovers."

Dennis had been listening intently and now he spoke up. "You know, when I was in Germany, I met two men who told me they had inside information about that fire in the Reichstag building in Berlin.

"Hitler and the Nazis said it was the Reds who did it, but these two guys knew for sure that it was just one Dutch Commie, because he was their friend. He tried to get them to help but they refused."

"The fire wasn't a Red conspiracy at all but Hitler used it to get more power," I said. "What if the Commies here deliberately murdered Winthrop just to make it into a RoBerTo conspiracy? They would be turning the Reichstag fire story upside down and using it for their own propaganda. It would be pretty clever, actually."

"This way they could get more power here in San Francisco," Dennis said.

The chief crossed his arms at his chest. "So you're saying the Nazis used the fire to get rid of the Reds in Berlin, and here the Reds are using the murder to get rid of — who? — we don't really have any serious Axis supporters in San Francisco."

"Eddie's paper and the Commie paper have been saying that the city government, the Catholic Church and the fascist movement are all one big conspiracy against the people.

"*The Reds* believe it." I shrugged. "Or they don't believe it and are just using it to get their people elected mayor and supervisors. Either way, it would be the kind of cynical tactics the Commies and fascists have used for twenty years now."

"They are still pushing that line," Dennis chimed in. "Look at the paper you just showed us, Chief, and remember there's another election coming up next year. The Red paper is already starting to say the mayor should be kicked out of office — he's a secret fascist and Mussolini gave him special medals in return for his loyalty."

"My head is swimming here," the chief said, "but I think your theory needs to be followed up, Dennis. It just so happens that I have someone who is keeping me informed about what's happening in the Red network here in the city. She's a good Catholic girl named Ruthie Adams. Let's bring her into this investigation. Let's see what she thinks of your idea."

"Okay, chief," I said. "Have her call me at home. We can meet her in my law office. That way nobody at the Hall will see that she's meeting with us."

"It's good to see you are just as smart as ever, Commissioner," O'Reilly said, but there was no good-natured kidding at all in his sharp edged tone of voice.

"Don't forget that we're still at the beginning of this case," I said. "With Easter holiday and all, we got a slow start, but we've already followed up on a couple of theories."

"Plus," Dennis said, leaning forward, his big frame dominating the front of the chief's desk, "we'll be looking into Harlan Winthrop's life now — the days before Palm Sunday and all his activities. It takes time, Chief."

"Get out of here, you two," O'Reilly said, frowning. "I don't need a police academy refresher course. And by the way, I assume you've already searched his house."

Dennis and I looked at each other, and I looked back at the chief. "We've been too busy chasing down possible leads related to the RoBerTo business. Of course, we'll do that."

The chief nodded and made a gesture shooing us out of the office. Dennis and I got up, said goodbye, and walked out of his office. We said good morning to Maggie McPherson.

It was only 8:30 in the morning and she looked tired.

I figured that she was at her wits end knowing she would have to cope with the chief's bad mood again today, another day of bussing the Japs out of the city.

Chapter 9   Tuesday, April 7, 1942

The telephone rang. We looked at each other, both probably wondering the same thing — should we get up and answer?

Flora and I were enjoying our favorite dessert, a cake made with lady finger cookies soaked in Tuaca and espresso, layered with a mixture of whipped cream, egg whites, sugar and mascarpone, topped with cocoa powder and chocolate shavings.

The recipe was passed down from Flora's great grandmother in the Veneto, and we like it with a glass of Moscato d'Asti from the Bosco family vineyard in the Piedmont.

The ringing continued for a while before Flora finally said, "I'll answer it, Tony, but I can't imagine who could be calling so late."

I heard her talking in the hallway. She put the receiver down on the shelf of the telephone niche and walked back to the dining room. She was smiling now, her eyes full of mischief.

"It's one of your women friends," she said. "She refused to tell me her name. She said it's a confidential matter. What's going on, Tony?"

Standing there like that, with her hands on her hips and color in her cheeks, I felt a surge of affection. It took me a minute to refocus my attention.

Talking on the telephone was now the furthest thing from my mind. "This is probably one of the chief's people, a woman named Miss Adams," I explained, before picking up the phone.

"Hello, this is Tony Bosco."

"Commissioner, this is Ruthie," said a melodious voice with a South of Market accent. "I hope it's not too late; your housekeeper seemed put out."

I cleared my throat. "That was not my housekeeper, it was my wife who answered."

"Yeah? Well, how about that? I hope I didn't say anything that upset her. The chief said this is some kind of 'hush, hush' business and I should say nothing to nobody and to only talk to you and some detective named Sullivan."

"Yes," I replied, "the matter is indeed confidential. I'm not at liberty to discuss it with you on the telephone."

"Well, *pardon me*, Mr. Commissioner, you don't have to get all high and mighty. The chief said it was urgent business and I should call right away. So what's so urgent, and why'd the chief want me to contact you?

"I have to go to a meeting with a bunch of communists tonight. If I'm late they'll want me to do confession and penance, Moscow style, again and I don't fancy it, so hurry up and tell me what you want."

"Miss Adams," I said, curious now to see what this brassy young woman looked like, "please come to my law office tomorrow morning at 9:00 AM.

"The chief will have already given you the address. I will be there with Detective Sullivan. We'll explain everything."

"I'll be there," she said. "Oh, and by the way call me Ruthie, never Miss Adams."

I walked back into the dining room and saw that Flora had poured herself another glass of Moscato d'Asti. She was reading the new *Time Magazine.* She looked up at me and asked if I would like some more wine.

"Yes, thank you," I said and she put down the magazine. Joe DiMaggio was on the back cover; six little pictures described the secret of his "mighty swing." There was also a photo of him dressed in a suit and tie, holding a cigarette, telling us that he liked Camels because they were milder, with 28% less nicotine.

"I wonder what they paid Joe for that endorsement," I said as Flora refilled my glass.

"Never mind Joe," she replied, "who was that woman and what was so important that she could so rudely refuse to tell me her name?"

"Well," I said, "you remember when the chief called the day after Palm Sunday and I went to see him at the Hall of Justice?"

"Oh, yes, you never told me what that was all about."

"I've been planning to tell you, but we've been so busy with Easter and all there's been no time. Actually, I need your advice about this, because it's a strange case. I'll tell you all about it tomorrow. The long and short of it is that I'm working with a young detective on a strange and unsettling murder case. The girl that just called will be helping us out."

"Somebody should teach her some manners," Flora joked.

"Maybe so, but she's got a lot of spirit." I stood up, leaned down and kissed her on the cheek. "And speaking of spirit, tomorrow will be here before we know it. Let's go upstairs."

She smiled up at me, and with a glint in her eye. "Yes, and who knows what the rest of today will bring?" she said.

Chapter 10   Wednesday April 8, 1942

The front doors opened up into the marble lobby. Customers were already lined up at the tellers' windows and it wasn't even 9:00. Several of them were young men in uniform. I reminded myself we have to stop calling this the Bank of Italy building.

I took the elevator to the seventh floor and saw a tall, beautiful woman wearing a red jacket, a black skirt, a white blouse, and a red beret standing outside my office door. She was reading the Sporting Green section of *The San Francisco Chronicle*.

Her thick, dark-brown hair swayed from side to side as she turned her large green eyes in my direction. There was a dramatic contrast between the color of her hair and beret and her pale unblemished complexion. Her full lips matched the color of her hat.

"You must be the boss," she said, with a large, cocky smile.

"Good morning," I said, smiling myself, "you must be Miss Adams."

"Boss, let's get one thing straight," she replied. "I'm Ruthie, just plain Ruthie. Never Miss Adams."

"I'll do my best to remember that," I said, opening the door and motioning her to go inside.

"If you're as persistent about your work as you are about how we're supposed to address you, I look forward to our association."

She frowned. "Where'd you learn to talk like that?" she asked. "I know a few lawyers. None of them talk so grand and highfalutin as you."

I closed the door and walked to my desk, where I put down my briefcase. "Here's some plain speaking," I said. "Why so sensitive about your name?"

"That is a long story. The short version is my parents named me Ruth Fuller Adams. Everybody called me Ruthie when I was little, and I liked that. But after my daddy ran off and left my mom and me, I decided nobody was going to call me by *his* name. So I'm Ruthie Fuller now."

"I'm sorry," I replied, "that must have been difficult for you and your mother."

"Yeah," she said. "It was for a while, but he was a bum and we never missed him. My mom got together with a swell fellow who loves her to death and takes good care of her. They aren't married, but I say, 'so what'? Being married didn't do anything for my mom except give her headaches and a bunch of black eyes."

I decided to change the subject. "The chief said something about you being 'a good Catholic girl' the other day. By your accent, I'm guessing you went to school at St. Patrick's or St. Joseph's."

"My mom and I love the chief, he's some kind of relative. But just between you and me, all that 'good Catholic girl' stuff is a bunch of malarkey. I'm a South of Market girl, for sure. I got my first communion at St. Joseph's Church. We lived around the corner on Tehama Street. At college, some of my teachers thought I was from Brooklyn, New York, but I told them this is how real people talk in San Francisco."

Dennis Sullivan had walked in as Ruthie was speaking. They gave each other the once over.

"So I guess you're real and I'm phony because I speak proper English?" he said. "Is that what you're trying to say?"

"You must be the detective the chief told me about," Ruthie answered. "But he didn't say I would be working with a tall, handsome guy with such a smart mouth!"

She put out her hand. "Hello, Detective, I'm Ruthie," she said.

He smiled. "Call me Dennis. What's all this about real people, anyway?"

"Ah, well, Mr. Matinee Idol copper, I'm just mouthing off with the boss here. Come to think of it, communists are always going on about how they're all for the people. But you get them drunk enough, they'll admit they're not for *all* the people."

"According to them," Dennis chimed in, "lawyers, bankers, cops, Catholics, hell pretty much anybody who owns a house or any kind of business and isn't a Commie — they aren't real people at all."

"Whether we are real or not," I said, "the three of us need to get down to work here. First of all, Ruthie, we have to bring you up to date about the case the chief asked us to investigate."

I explained it all to her: the stabbing, the sign, and everything we'd done so far.

"Now," I said, "we're working on another theory — that the Commies have done away with Harlan Winthrop to kill two birds with one stone: they rid themselves of one of their worst enemies and discredit the city government, the police and the Church, saying they're, well *we're*, in cahoots with the fascists."

"And you want me to check out your theory using my connections, is that it?" Ruthie asked. "What makes you think they would let the cat out of the bag to me? I'm just a nobody. I do courier work for them. I take notes at meetings. Sometimes I translate stuff from Russian to English, stuff that comes from

Moscow, or they want to write a letter to Moscow in Russian and none of the big boys are around."

"You must have a lot of connections if you've done all this work," I said.

She shrugged. "I guess so. You know, a lot of these party big shots, they have names like Smith or Jones, but they actually came from Russia, or Finland, or Lithuania or somewhere back there in Europe. They change their name so they can fit in better. But a lot of 'em go back and forth all the time — well they can't now with the war and all, but they did right up til Pearl Harbor."

"You can read and write Russian?" Dennis asked, sounding incredulous.

"Sure I can," Ruthie said. "You think just because I'm a good looking broad I don't have any brains? You might look intelligent, Detective, and you're wearing a smart suit, but maybe you're as thick as all the other cops I've met."

Dennis looked surprised. "Hold on," he said, but Ruthie ignored him.

"You think a girl has to be ugly and wearing eyeglasses to be smart. Well, my Phi Beta Kappa key from the university is just as shiny as anybody else's, and it's for majoring in Eastern European languages, not home economics."

"I'm sure Dennis meant nothing insulting toward you," I said. "No doubt there are very few women, or men for that matter, who can read and write Russian around here. We both are impressed by your skills, and I'm sure that goes for the communists, too."

"Yeah, sure," she replied, "whatever you say. But they're never going to sit down and tell me all their secrets. And for sure, if they murdered some big shot banker, that's not something they're telling every Tom, Dick, and Harry or little Ruthie."

"You're not so little," Dennis said. "You're taller than Tony. In fact I wouldn't be surprised if you played girls' basketball at the university."

"Good deduction, Detective!" she replied, "Maybe I got a little hot under the collar there. You might make a good detective after all, Dennis. Yeah, I played for the Bears at UC."

"See — after all we three have a great deal in common," I said. "Dennis and I both played for the Gaels, and you for the Bears! So let's put our heads together and figure out how we can devise a play and win this one for the chief."

"Devise a play!" Ruthie exclaimed. "There you go again talking like somebody up there on Nob Hill!

"What you're really saying is you want me to sneak around and rat on my friends who happen to be communists. Like that guy Gypo in the movie a few years ago."

"That was *The Informer*," Dennis said. "It won four Oscars."

"Yeah, that's the one," Ruthie replied. "They killed him, the IRA, right? They hated him, and he hated himself. Everybody hates a rat. But I'm not worried about ratting out my friends. None of them would murder anybody, not even a banker!"

"We would never ask you to do something you thought was morally wrong, but we *are* trying to find a *murderer* here," I said. "Whoever killed Harlan Winthrop took the life of a man who was working hard to help win this war against the Axis. They stabbed him in the back!"

Dennis said, "I was in Germany and I met guys who told me their former comrades sentenced them to death after they went back to the Church and spoke out against the Communist Party.

They asked me to help them come to America. They were running scared.

"They told me if they stayed in Germany, they would never be safe."

"Precisely," I said. "And look what happened to Leon Trotsky down in Mexico City — a Red agent axed him to death. Josef Stalin gave the killer a medal!

"Ruthie, I'm sure none of your friends are murderers, but what if some other Reds or a Commie agent killed Harlan Winthrop? What if they're willing to use murder to get back at Harlan and his banker friends and to discredit our government? Don't you have a duty to help us find that out?"

Dennis said, "Maybe this theory is full of holes, but we won't know until we check it out."

"I get it, you guys. I'm already helping out the chief, making sure he knows what's going on with the Reds. I don't belong to the CP, but I like a lot of what the party does. I told the chief that I'm smart enough to know it's not a perfect outfit, and my friends know that, too."

"Do they know about your connection with Chief O'Reilly?" I asked.

"Of course they do, and they'd rather have me working for the chief than somebody who really hates communists."

"Sounds pretty complicated, if you ask me," Dennis said.

"Yeah, I suppose, but I know that none of my friends in the CP would murder anybody, not even if the party ordered them to do it."

"Let's do this," I said. "Let's walk over to Fosters Cafeteria on Sansome Street, have some coffee and donuts, and let this all percolate for a little while. Ruthie, do you have time?"

"Okay," she said, "lead the way, boss."

Chapter 11   Wednesday, April 8, 1942

The aroma of fried food and the noise of conversation and clattering dishes filled the air. The place was bustling with the usual crowd of financial district clerks and secretaries, delivery truck drivers, and construction workers. They were digging into hearty breakfasts of pancakes, waffles, and bacon and eggs with Fosters' famous home fried potatoes. A table of bleary-eyed servicemen in disheveled uniforms were trying to sober up after a night of debauchery at the International Settlement on Pacific Street.

We lined up at the counter with our trays, picked out donuts and filled our cups with coffee. I paid the cashier and we sat down at one of the few empty tables, stirring our coffee and nibbling our donuts until Dennis broke the ice. "Ruthie, how is it you got involved doing the work you are doing for the chief? I don't imagine you answered a help wanted ad in the paper."

"Well, it's not because I'm one hundred percent against everything that the communists are doing," she replied. "A lot of good people support their work to improve things for working people, especially Negroes.

"When I was a student, the communists at Berkeley went all out to help with the farmworkers down in the Valley. Nobody else came even close to them. Me and my friend Barbara, Barbara O'Connell — well she got married so now she's Barbara O'Connell Bates — we drove down there to Salinas with food and medicine after the owners and the police attacked them.

"Barbara joined and she's in charge of all the communist education programs now. We used to be great pals but she couldn't understand why I wouldn't join up. We had some big fights about it."

"Why did you not want to join, if you thought the Commies were doing such good work?" Dennis asked.

"I never liked the way they treated us. Always talking down to us and acting like we were dummies just because we were girls. Barbara said it didn't matter, that all men act that way, but I said if you Reds say you believe everybody should be equal, how come that doesn't include women?"

She stirred her coffee. "Also, the communists have done terrible things to get power and once they have power they are ruthless! We know how Stalin killed thousands of peasants who refused to go along with his farming program. And we know he ordered the murder of Trotsky.

"I could never be part of a bunch that does killing like that. How can anybody justify murdering thousands of people? That it's all okay because in the end the world will be a swell place to live in?"

I agreed. "I think Stalin killed a lot more than thousands in Russia. And what about how he turned on other leftists, killing hundreds of them in Barcelona during the Spanish Civil War?"

"My Hungarian professor told me another story like that," Ruthie said. "Dr. Szasz, who was a teacher in a Catholic school in Budapest when Bela Kun took over in 1919.

"One morning, a bunch of guys — the Lenin Boys — marched into the school. Leather jackets, guns, clubs, the whole shebang. They pulled the principal out of his office, marched him to the sixth floor and threw him out of a window!

"What's his crime? He's the head of a Catholic School! They beat up all of the teachers, lined some of them up against a wall in the yard, and shot them like dogs.

"Professor Szasz and his family escaped. They went to London. Then he was invited to teach at Berkeley. He told me Bela Kun 'got his just desserts' because Stalin executed him after one of those show trials a couple of years ago."

"I take it your friend Barbara is willing to accept the Red line of 'the end justifies the means?'" I asked. "Are you still friends, or did you and she stop seeing each other?"

"We're still friends, but now she's more of a friend to me than I am to her. She says the party wouldn't approve of our friendship, but, listen, we both grew up in the same neighborhood. We go back a long way. We went to different high schools, but we were in college at the same time, and we took Russian classes together.

"When we went back and forth to Salinas to help out with the strike down there, I met another Party member I befriended. She grew up in New York and Los Angeles, but she's the same age as me and Barbara. Her name is Esther Green — since she got married Esther Green Yokota. Her husband Larry is also a party member.

"Esther, Larry, Barbara and I like each other and have a good time together. We're not going to stop being friends because the party frowns on them getting together with somebody like me."

I nodded. "So when you were talking about not wanting to be a rat and inform on your friends, you were talking about Barbara and Esther and Larry, is that what you meant?"

Ruthie frowned and drained her cup. "Yeah, that's exactly what I meant."

"So, you said your friends in the CP know you are working for the chief," Dennis said. "They accept you anyway. But what if other communists find out? Aren't you worried that they'll blow the whistle on you? Or do you think the bond you all have is so strong that they would approve?"

"That's too many questions, Detective," Ruthie replied. "You're making me feel like I'm getting the third degree here!"

Ruthie pulled off her beret and put it in her lap. She stabbed the air with her index finger. "Look, it's hard to explain, but just take my word. The communists I know are doing good work to make this country better. Yeah, I've heard all the bad stuff about Stalin but I know he's fighting Hitler now. For now, that's good enough for me.

"The way I see it," she sat back in her chair, "the kind of information I pass on to the chief isn't about any particular people. That's why I kind of blew up when I thought you wanted me to inform on my friends.

"Let me give you an example of what I do. Back in August, Mrs. McWilliams, you know, the judge's wife, told me that she was part of a big group of people who were planning one of those mass meetings in the Civic Auditorium. She's an old friend of my mom's. She and a bunch of other gals from the Catholic Ladies Association helped the families during the big Salinas lettuce strike I told you about.

"So the chief says, 'Ruthie, can you go to that meeting, take notes for me and the archbishop, so we can see what kind of speeches people are giving?' The chief told me that one of the officers in this 'Citizens Committee for American-Allied Defense' is a Russian guy who's a Communist big shot. He's a teacher at the art school in North Beach, Victor Arnautoff."

"Didn't Arnautoff paint those murals in Coit Tower?" Dennis asked

"He painted the big one that you see when you walk in the door," I said. "He was the director of that whole mural-painting project."

"That's right," Ruthie said. "And by the way, I'm a secretary in the office at the art school. I work there about twenty hours a week. So I know Arnautoff and all those other artistic types. He's a swell guy; we talk Russian all the time. He was one of the guys who painted the walls in Coit Tower. The chief especially wanted to know what Arnautoff was saying, as well as the main speaker named Walter Duranty. The chief asked me to especially write down anything Duranty said about whether the Stalin government is doing a good job over there.

"So I sat there surrounded by hundreds of folks, scribbling away in my notebook, and the next day I gave my notebook to one of the cops who lives near me in North Beach, and he passed it on to the chief. I've gone to a lot of these kinds of meetings. They're kind of fun, sometimes, but usually they're really boring.

"And sometimes I do volunteer stuff for Barbara, Larry, and Esther. A lot of people are like me; we all help out with stuff we think is good work, but we'd never join up."

"Ruthie," I said, "I'm beginning to see how you can help us with our investigation. What if you just go on with your life as you have been doing, say for the next couple of weeks or so, and keep your ears peeled for anything you hear that might relate to the Harlan Winthrop murder? I think you should avoid asking a bunch of questions; that might lead your friends to wonder what's going on."

"Also," Dennis said, "from the way you described your friends, it sounds like they would definitely condemn murder, even of an influential banker like Winthrop. How did they react when Ramón Mercader killed Leon Trotsky?"

"They were horrified," Ruthie said. "And so was I. In fact, we had a big discussion about it, because their official party meeting voted for a resolution that praised the killing because Trotsky was a so-called enemy of the state."

Ruthie put her beret back on and got up from the table. "Okay, gentlemen, how's *this* for a plan — I'll just go on as usual with my eyes and ears open. I'm going to call Professor Szasz, too. He might have some ideas about all of this, if that's okay with you, boss."

"That's a good idea," I said.

"All right. A week from now, I'll meet with you here again at 10:30. I'll give you a report about anything I've heard that seems connected to who killed this guy."

Chapter 12   Sunday, April 12, 1942

I didn't have to wait a week to hear from Ruthie.

We were having Sunday lunch after Mass when the telephone rang and Flora answered. "That's Mrs. McCaughey calling long distance from Los Angeles," she guessed "We're working together on the Catholic women's war bond drive."

After a few minutes of talking, I heard her put the receiver down on the shelf. When she came back to the living room, she said, "It's for you, Tony, Miss Fuller. She sounded very upset."

I untucked my napkin, put it next to my plate, got up from the table and went to answer the telephone.

"Hello, Ruthie," I said. "I didn't expect to hear from you so soon. My wife said you sounded upset."

"Your wife sounds like a smart woman, boss. When do I get to meet her? I am kinda upset, she's right.

"I called because something terrible has happened and I don't know what to do. I need to talk to you as soon as possible. Can you meet me here?"

"Meet you? Where? What's the matter?" I asked.

"I'm at the Riviera. Do you know it? I had a martini to steady my nerves but I just got more upset. I didn't want to call you, especially on a Sunday, but I don't know anybody else I can turn to."

"I know the Riviera. If you mean the restaurant in North Beach. We sometimes go there for dinner with friends. If it's an emergency of some kind, I can be there in a half hour."

"I'll wait in the cocktail lounge," she said.

"I'll be there as soon as I can," I promised, "but please don't drink another martini!"

The receiver went dead, so I hung up and went back to the dining room. Flora had already cleared away the dishes and silverware. She was in the kitchen with her hands in a sink full of soapy water.

"At least she had enough manners to tell me her name this time," Flora said, "but seriously, what happened to her? I could tell there was something wrong."

"She's all upset about something that happened," I explained. "She says she needs advice and she wanted to tell me about it in person this afternoon so I told her I would meet her."

"Well, of course. You should do what you think best, Tony. She sounds young and she probably senses that you're a good listener."

"She is young, that's for sure, and she told me that she grew up without a father."

"Well, there you go. Go take off that tie, put on a sport shirt and a nice sport coat and go help her."

I went upstairs to the bedroom and did what she suggested. When I came back into the kitchen, I kissed her on the check, and said goodbye.

"It's just after 3:00," I said, "I should be back by supper."

I left my car at the valet stand outside the restaurant with a pimply blond kid who looked barely old enough to drive. I guess all the regulars have enlisted already.

"How old are you?" I asked him as he walked up to my window.

"I got my license six months ago, grandpa, and I'm a good driver," he wisecracked. "Don't worry, I'll take good care of this beautiful Buick for you."

After the sunshine outside, it took a few seconds for my eyes to adjust to the dimly-lit cocktail lounge. I noticed people on the banquettes, but paid them no mind after locating Ruthie. She was sitting by herself at the bar, a cigarette in one hand and a cocktail glass in the other.

She noticed me, put her glass down, put out the cigarette and slipped off the bar stool. "Tony, I'm so glad to see you!" she said in an excited voice.

"It took me longer than I expected," I replied, walking up to her. "Lombard Street was clogged with military vehicles. I ended up making a big detour and drove over Russian Hill on Union Street."

She stepped up to me and grabbed the lapels of my jacket with both hands. "The military, the military! Why did they force us into this war?"

I was taken aback and gently pried her hands off me, stepping away. "Ruthie, what's happened?" I said, "Here, sit down."

I walked us over to the closest banquette and gently sat her down, before taking a seat next to her.

"Why are you so upset?" I asked.

She started crying. Several people, including the bartender, were looking our way.

"Bartender," I called, "bring us a glass of water, please."

Ruthie looked up at me and slowly stopped sobbing. I took the handkerchief out of my lapel pocket and handed it to her.

She wiped her eyes.

"Oh, Tony," she said, "thanks for meeting me. I don't usually get so emotional about things, but I knew I could trust you and didn't know who else to turn to. It's this damned war!

"I've been worried sick for two whole days, ever since General King surrendered to the Japanese at Bataan. The *Examiner* quoted the Japanese army saying they were going to *exterminate* the enemy. My cousin Patrick is fighting with that army! I don't know if he is still alive! He could be wounded, or a prisoner — Oh, God, this is so terrible!" She started crying again.

The bartender gave me a quizzical look as he handed me the glass of water. "Everything's fine," I said to him, nodding my head toward the bar and he walked away.

I gave the glass to Ruthie and said, "Take a drink, and then take some deep breaths. You're right to be worried, but your cousin would want you to be brave, I'm sure.

"I've been thinking these last months, the Japanese may well start bombing us here if they keep up their victories. We have to be strong the way the Londoners were during the Blitz. Like the man said in a broadcast I heard — we must simply go on, or we'll go under."

"Oh, Tony," she said, calming down. "I know you're right, but I've hardly slept at all for two days now. I keep seeing images in my mind from those newsreels of what the Japanese soldiers did in Nanking. What will become of Patrick?"

I sighed. "We can't know," I said, "we simply have to pray for him and carry on with our work here. I hope it doesn't sound callous, but he's in God's hands now."

I stood up. "Come on, let's get you something to eat."

I helped her up, and we walked into the restaurant. The late afternoon rays shone through the large windows, lighting up the framed watercolor paintings of French resorts. A smattering of early diners were talking and eating while a gray-haired waiter with a long sad face came right to the table we headed for, pulled out a chair for Ruthie, and handed us two menus.

"Bring us some bread and butter right away and two glasses of water," I said.

As he went on his way, Ruthie looked at me and said, "I'm not hungry, and I don't feel well." Her eyes were red and her face blotchy from crying,

"You'll feel better after you've eaten something," I assured her.

The waiter arrived with a basket of the Riviera's famous sourdough bread, cut into slices, along with a small dish with butter. "Pretty soon we won't be able to serve you butter like this, guv," he said to me in a nasal voice, "we're bound to have rationing, you know." He turned to Ruthie, then to me. "Have you decided what to order?"

"How would you like some soup, Ruthie?" I asked. She didn't answer, so I ordered two bowls of the Marseilles clam chowder.

The waiter scribbled it down in his notebook. "Coming right up," he said.

After he left, I handed Ruthie a slice of buttered bread. She took it from me and bit off a piece of crust and bread together like a true San Franciscan. Tourists tended to eat the bread and leave the hard crusts.

"People come from all over the country for the clam chowder and sourdough bread at the Riviera," I said, trying to lighten the mood. "They even got a mention in that big new guidebook that our Downtown Association put out with money from the WPA."

Ruthie seemed to perk up a little. "Oh, a bunch of my friends wrote some sections for that book. They were glad at the chance to earn good money just by writing up little reports about different neighborhoods."

The waiter returned with a tray bearing two steaming bowls of clam chowder. Pieces of potato and clams were sticking out of the reddish colored broth. After he put down the bowls, he slipped the tray under his arm and one by one picked up the napkins beside our plates, shook them open, and handed them to us. He asked if we wanted anything else. When I said we didn't he wished us "bon appetite" and walked away.

Ruthie took another piece of bread from the basket and buttered it. "You're right, Tony, I feel better already," she said. "I guess I shouldn't have ordered that third martini after all. By the time you arrived, I had the blues really bad!"

I smiled. "I'm glad to hear you're starting to feel better. After we finish here, I can take you home in my car. Once you catch up on your sleep, you're bound to feel much better.

"If you'd like, we could stop at Saints Peter and Paul to say a prayer for your cousin Patrick and all the other soldiers who surrendered. And for all the others who are still fighting in Corregidor, too."

"That's nice of you, but I'm not going home. I'm going to see Esther and Larry this evening."

"Ah, yes, your Commie friends," I said.

"Tony, I don't like it when you and Dennis say 'Commies' like you do, or 'Reds.' It sounds disrespectful, you know?"

"I suppose you're right. As we lawyers like to say, I take your point."

She smiled. "Ah, sure, as my mom would say, and aren't you the gentleman!

"I promised to go over tonight and help them send out notices about a meeting of the Friends of the Soviet Union. We all sit around their kitchen table, fold the notices, put them in envelopes, seal and address and stamp the envelopes. We have a good time and afterwards have coffee and cookies. The worst part is licking the stamps. They taste awful!"

I started to say "that's a Commie outfit" but stopped myself at the last minute.

Ruthie laughed. I was happy to see humor in her green eyes once more.

"Ruthie," I said, "I know you are upset today, but I wonder if you might keep your eyes and ears open when you are with your friends about anything that might relate to that murder on Palm Sunday."

"Oh, yeah, sure I can. But I have an idea," she said. "Could you meet Esther and Larry and maybe help them? They're upset about the evacuation; their date is April 30. They are right in the middle of the move-out, which is supposed to end on May 20. The problem is that Esther is White and Larry is Japanese and so far they were told that Esther will have to stay here when Larry and Joan, their little girl, have to go to a camp."

"But the Army promised to keep families all together," I said. "It would be a terrible immoral act for the Army to take fathers by force from their wives and children!"

"The Army doesn't care," she said, "at least that's what they were told. Also, Larry was born in California, and he wants to enlist, but they won't let him.

"Could you talk to them? You know the chief, you were a Police Commissioner, and I know you are the head of one of the Draft Boards in San Francisco. Maybe you could 'say a word' to the right person and help them!"

I shook my head. I felt bad that a family would be separated like this, but I knew that General DeWitt was proud of his "no exceptions" policy. The Christian part of me genuinely wanted to help, and the lawyer part of me was also working — if I *did* succeed in convincing the General to keep their family intact, then Esther and Larry might take me into their confidence and tell me if they knew about a connection between the Reds and the murder of Harlan Winthrop. A little *Quid Pro Quo* never hurt anybody.

"Ruthie," I said, "I'd be happy to talk with them. I could drive you to their home after we finish eating. You can introduce us, and they can give me all their details. I could start telephoning my connections tomorrow morning."

I ordered coffee and after we finished I called for the check.

While we were waiting I heard a loud voice calling, "*Signor Bosco!*"

I turned to see Eddie Sarno. "*Avvocato,*" he shouted, his shiny brown suit wrinkled, his tie askew. He'd come into the restaurant from the cocktail lounge with three men, all dressed the same as him. His companions stood awkwardly as he walked up to our table.

"I saw you comforting your girlfriend in the lounge," he said. "I'm glad to see you've made up and are now enjoying yourselves. I wish you a very pleasant evening together." He winked.

"C'mon, Eddie, leave them at peace," one of his companions said. "Let's sit down."

Ruthie had gone pale. My pulse was pounding. I took several bills from my wallet, left them on top of our check, and got up to leave. "I'll explain all this after we leave," I said to Ruthie.

Chapter 13 Sunday, April 12, 1942

I didn't like the knowing smirk on the face of the valet kid as he opened the door for Ruthie, so I tipped him a nickel instead of a dime. It wasn't until we passed St. Mary's Cathedral on Van Ness that I realized I needed to telephone Flora to tell her I wouldn't be home for supper.

I parked in one of the reserved spaces outside the City Hall and flipped down my sun visor so my Commissioner's permit was visible. Ruthie waited for me in the car as I went across the street to use one of the phone booths in the lobby of the Civic Auditorium.

The Civic Center was full of boys in uniforms. A lot of them were with even younger girls wearing lots of makeup and colorful outfits. A crowd of several hundred people were milling around admiring one of those new Sherman tanks on display next to the USO center.

I kept the call short and told Flora I'd fill her in at home. "I'll fix you something later if you are hungry," she said.

"You've been quiet since we left the restaurant. What was all that about with that loudmouth guy?" Ruthie asked when I got back in the car.

"Eddie Sarno hates the Church," I explained. "He claims it's Mussolini's partner, so any good Catholic is a fascist — a wolf in sheep's clothing. He knows I'm active in the Catholic Men's Association, so in his book I'm the enemy."

"Anybody with half a brain knows not all Catholics, even Italian Catholics, are fascists," Ruthie said. "It'd be like saying everybody who wants justice for the working class is a communist."

"Yes, I know," I said, "but people are not always logical when it comes to religion and politics, wouldn't you agree?"

"Oh, but I'm *always* logical," she said, her sense of humor making a comeback.

I chuckled. "Also, he knows I raised a lot of money to build four new shrines inside Saints Peter and Paul, the Italian Cathedral. More people are coming to church there than ever before. He can't stand that and ridicules Italians who go to church. Now he says they're traitors to our country."

"My cousin Patrick has an Italian Uncle named Matthew," Ruthie said. "Matthew says he loves Italy like a mother, but he's married to America. He's loyal to his mother until his mother disrespects his wife, and after that he takes his wife's side. All three of Matthew's sons enlisted the day after Pearl Harbor."

"Matthew is a wise man," I said. "I agree with him one hundred percent. The other thing is that Eddie has it in for the police department and anybody associated with it in any way. He believes the police are just a bunch of goons working for the ruling class, always oppressing the people."

"Speak of the devil," Ruthie said. "What's that paddy wagon doing there?" She pointed to a black van, its back doors open, parked in front of the Hibernia Bank. Next to it stood a beat cop.

"There's probably another fight between servicemen and civilians," I replied. "See the line of men waiting to enter the President Follies burlesque theater?"

"ANN CORIO, THE SWAMP WOMAN," the marquee announced in large white letters

"Last week, a fight broke out when a sailor said he didn't like standing in line next to an 'Eye-Talian.' The man in question slugged him and broke his nose. Their friends jumped in and then there was a regular brawl until the cops broke it up. They arrested eleven people for disturbing the peace.

"The mayor and I have tried for years to close down these establishments, but the theater owners and the customers have too much influence with the Board of Supervisors."

"That's such an old fashioned fuss feathers idea," Ruthie said. "I'm surprised you would say that. Why be such a spoil sport? Those guys are going off to fight for us, they should at least be able to have some fun before they leave! They're not hurting anybody!"

"I don't agree with you, Ruthie. Burlesque shows are the exploitation of young women by predatory theater owners."

"There you go again, with your high and mighty talk. You don't get to have the last word, Commissioner," she said. "If a woman wants to use her God-given endowments to make a living and please her fans, I say 'more power to her!'"

"Please don't get angry just because we disagree," I said. "You need to give me directions to the home of your friends. You said it was in Japantown and we're almost there."

"I usually go to Esther and Larry's on the Geary Street streetcar. I've never come this way before," Ruthie said.

I was driving along Fulton Street to Japantown. We passed several blocks of fifty-year-old two and three story wooden houses, all needing paint. "The big fire in '06 never got this far west," I said. "The owners of these old wrecks live somewhere else and rent them out. The health department had to close some of them down."

"What's that huge streamline thing on the left up ahead?"

Ruthie asked.

"That's the Acme Beer bottling plant. They just had the grand opening two weeks ago."

"It's taking up the whole block. I've never seen anything this modern before, just in magazines!"

"Yes," I said. "It has five stories, but you can't tell because all you see is this huge thing the size of a large airplane hangar that's all rounded off on the edges and the roof, and covered with a sort of continuous skin made of glass bricks. There's nothing like it in San Francisco."

"It's kind of beautiful the way it glows in the sunset, isn't it?" she said. "I like it."

Every block showed signs of the Army's evacuation of Japantown and every other place where Japanese people lived or were doing business. The Kisen Company store had signs covering both windows: "Closing Out Sale" and "50% Off" and "Everything Must Go." The Tokyo Fish Market windows were covered with brown paper. Someone had nailed a large sign on the door frame: "For Lease, Coldwell Banker Realty Company, 57 Sutter Street, SUtter 5420"

"We're pretty close," Ruthie said. "Turn right here and then you can park anywhere in the next few blocks. It's a sort of little alley, I'll show you."

As we parked and got out, I wondered if my car would still be there when I came back. Most of the cars were more than ten years old; a few hadn't been new since well before the Great Crash in '29.

I followed Ruthie into a space between two small 1890s houses. It led to an elongated courtyard around which stood another half dozen equally venerable small dwellings. They had a decrepit look about them. The Victorian writers Flora loves to read would probably put them to use as picturesque sites of romantic trysts. I wondered if they had indoor plumbing.

Ruthie stopped in front of a small wooden house that had been turned into two apartments, one upstairs and one downstairs. An unpainted wooden outside stairway led to the upstairs door. We ducked under it and Ruthie knocked on the door of the lower unit.

A tiny woman wearing an apron, with twinkling blue eyes and a large smile on her face opened the door and said, "Ruthie, hello!" She had to look up; Ruthie stood almost a foot taller.

"Hello, Esther," she said. "This is my new boss Tony Bosco, you know, the Police Commissioner. I'm working for him and a detective named Sullivan on a special project."

Esther came toward me and put out her hand. As I shook it, she turned her head sideways and looked at Ruthie with a mock serious expression. "Really, Ruthie? Commissioner Anthony Bosco? Mayor Rossi's 'Right Hand Man'?

"Larry," she called, "Come quick, here's a real live Capitalist-Imperialist Stooge of the Ruling Class!"

A handsome Japanese man in his mid-thirties wearing work clothes, his sleeves rolled up, came to the door.

"Commissioner Bosco," he said quietly, "welcome to our humble apartment. If Ruthie is working with you, she must trust you. If Ruthie trusts you, so do we." His handshake was firm and dry and his hand was hard and strong, undoubtedly from years of manual labor.

Ruthie broke the spell starting to walk inside. "Tony wants to talk to you both about the evacuation," she said. "I told him about your dilemma. He promises to try to help you keep your family together."

We walked directly into a small living room and then through a short hallway with a door to the bathroom on the left. The kitchen was on the right. In the back of the kitchen, a closed door most likely led to the bedroom. The table was covered with letter size stacks of the event posters. Boxes of envelopes were stacked on the floor.

"Joanie is asleep already, so you won't get to meet our darling daughter," Esther said to me. "If you could see her you would understand why we simply can't imagine separating the family."

Larry moved the stacks of posters off the table and pulled out one of the chairs. "Please sit down, Commissioner," he said. "Would you like a glass of water, or coffee?"

I declined. "Please call me Tony," I said. "I should be clear, as I said to Ruthie, I'm not sure that I can help you, but I believe no family should be separated, ever, and if there's anything I can do I will surely do it."

"Tony, I know you are Catholic," Esther said, "and I know you were one of the campaign managers for Mayor Rossi in the last election. Larry and I are both members of the Communist Party. We worked very hard to stop Angelo Rossi from being elected. Our newspaper published a number of articles very critical of you and the mayor. Our 'Party Line' as we call it says Catholics are our 'class enemies.' Do you really think you can ignore all of our differences to help us keep our family together?"

"We are living in a very different world today compared to 1939," I answered. "We are all allies now focused on defeating fascism and Japanese militarism, right?"

Larry put down the flyers in his hand and put his arm around Esther. He nodded in agreement.

"God meant families to be like little societies — independent of government, living according to the teachings of Christ. For the government to pull your family apart, that is a violation of God's law. You know that saying 'Render to Caesar what is Caesar's and to God what is God's.'"

Ruthie caught my eye and grimaced. Then she swept her right hand across her neck signaling that it was time to "cut" the speech.

I wasn't done and continued. "I happen to know that J. Edgar Hoover and the FBI believe this evacuation ordered by the President and the Army is unnecessary and undesirable. Hoover already has his lists of possibly subversive Japanese, Germans, and Italians. The FBI is watching them."

Smiling, I turned to Larry. "You and I are most likely on those lists right now!"

"That would not surprise me at all," Larry said. "But I'm a patriotic American. The Communist Party thinks I'm suspect and they suspended me! The Black Dragon Society says I am a traitor to the Emperor.

"But I believe strongly that all Americans must support our war effort against the Axis. I have already tried to enlist, but so far the Army has refused to consider it."

"Larry was born here in California," Esther said. "He went to school in Japan. So he has language skills and knowledge that could be a big help to our forces. If there's anything you can do to help get him signed up, that would be wonderful."

"Of course," I said, "that's perfectly logical. Just like we need as many native Italian speakers as we can get to send behind the lines and bring down Mussolini from within."

"Tony," Esther said, "I'd like to believe that you see helping us as a way to do a good deed. I don't mean you any disrespect here, but I'm Jewish. I can't help being suspicious. The Pope made those deals with Hitler and Mussolini. We all know he has hardly done *anything* to stop those two monsters from murdering Jews."

"I understand," I said, "I wish the Pope had done more. I wish he'd speak out now. But our Archbishop Mitty here in San Francisco, and my friend Archbishop Hanna before him — they both have been great friends to the Jews. Archbishop Mitty even spoke out against the attacks on Jewish synagogues and businesses and Jewish people back in November 1938. On a national radio broadcast!"

"I don't think we can make Tony responsible for what the Church has done or not done, can we?" Ruthie said. "That doesn't seem fair."

"I agree," Larry said. "But as communists, we like to think of all the angles. Like Esther, I don't mean any disrespect, Tony, but what's in it for you? Are you going to expect something in return?"

Larry and Esther should have been lawyers, I thought to myself.

"I don't expect anything at all," I assured them. "Tomorrow morning, I'm going to start working to make sure that your family stays together.

"But let me ask you a question. Do you have any reason to believe that any of your colleagues — I guess you call them your comrades — are working as part of a sort of fifth column here in San Francisco?

"As you rightly say, I'm an unofficial advisor to the mayor, and we want to keep the city as safe and secure as possible. It's our way of helping the war effort and keeping fear at a minimum."

"We are with you one hundred percent on that," Esther said. "One of my Party jobs is to fight back against anybody in our membership, and in any workplaces, who would support a wildcat strike now that we need to go all out and avoid any and all work stoppages."

Larry nodded. "I don't know of anybody who wants to interfere with the war effort by doing anything along the lines of a fifth column — sabotage, work slowdowns, criticizing the military, and strikes. In fact, our comrade Barry Rhodes, president of the dockworkers union, and his vice president Lewis Geldorf, they even put together a sort of truce between the CIO unions and the Chamber of Commerce. They call it the Homefront Friends for the Duration project. And Mack Kelly, the head of the AFL unions, signed on, too."

"Do you think Rhodes and Geldorf would meet with me?" I asked. "I'd like to know more about this project. I don't think the mayor has any idea this is happening. He would be reassured if I could tell him about it."

"I don't see why not," Esther answered. "Maybe then Mayor Rossi would let up on all of his 'The Reds this, and the Commies that' stuff.'"

Ruthie looked at me out of the corner of her eye, and I nodded slightly with a smile.

Chapter 14   Sunday, April 12, 1942

left Ruthie with Esther and Larry and got home about 10:30. Flora was still up.

"Would you like anything to eat?' she asked.

"Yes, thank you, I'm famished."

While she was cooking a frittata with onions, asparagus, and grated Stravecchio cheese, I opened a bottle of Chianti Classico and started telling her all about the Coit Tower case, Dennis Sullivan, and Ruthie. We were finishing the last of the wine when I told her about going to Japantown.

"The chief assigned Ruthie to work with me and Dennis. She has connections with the Reds and she took me to meet two Communist Party members named Esther and Larry. They live in a tiny apartment in a rundown building next to Japantown. The place is cramped but it's clean as a whistle and neat as a pin."

"Why shouldn't their house be clean?" Flora asked. "communists are people, too, aren't they?"

"Yes, actually they're charming people — thoughtful, and humorous, too. They have a little girl. The Army wants to separate them. They want to send Larry and the girl to a detention camp. Esther is White and Larry is a Japanese man born in California."

"It sounds like you expected them to have horns and a pointed tail!"

"I know, but I guess I thought they might be more like Eddie Sarno — nasty and sarcastic — attacking me every time we have ever run into each other."

"Eddie Sarno? Tony, you don't understand. Eddie acts like that not just because he's a devout Red and you're a practicing Catholic! Sure, that's part of it. But it's mostly because you are *Piemontese*! And you graduated from college and law school!

"I know you're going to say that you have never acted superior around him, but it's not what you have done but what he feels inside himself! He's from *Campania*. Even though he's an editor and a publisher, he feels like an outsider here. That's why he writes all those terrible things about you and Mario and A.P. Giannini."

"I should have thought of that," I said. "We're all from the North, and that makes us automatically suspect in Eddie's mind."

I told Flora about Eddie accosting us at the restaurant and about Ruthie's being devastated.

"She doesn't know if her cousin Patrick is dead or alive."

"How terrible for her," Flora said. "I would be shattered too, if you were in that situation. We should include them both in our prayers tonight, Tony."

I thought about the possibility of Esther and Larry working as allies the next morning while we had our cappuccino and toast. We talked about inviting Dennis and Ruthie to our house, then Flora said, "Go upstairs and start calling your friends so you can help our new Communist acquaintances keep their family together."

I went to my office and made my first call of the day to the chief. O'Reilly listened to my account of my meeting with Esther and Larry Yokota and I asked him to sign an appeal that will go to General DeWitt.

"I see what you're trying to do, but I can't put my name to something the papers could play up as me failing to put the security of the people of San Francisco ahead of a — well, frankly

— a couple of Commies. Even worse, a mixed-race couple, one of them a Jew. And what are you and Sullivan doing? I need a report. Harlan Winthrop is still in cold storage and we don't seem any closer to figuring out who put him there!" Again, he hung up without saying goodbye. It seemed to be turning into a habit.

District Attorney Shrader didn't hang up on me, but he wasted no time in telling me he didn't want to get involved either. "I agree with the General — a Jap is a Jap and we can't trust them."

But Joseph and Martin Schmitz offered to do anything I thought would help. They thanked me, again, for having agreed several months ago to campaign for Martin when he runs against Shrader in the next election for District Attorney. They offered to contact all of the members of their Order of Cincinnatus reform caucus in the County Democratic Party.

County Sheriff Fogarty and John Dolan, the Assistant U.S. Attorney, agreed with me that the whole evacuation program was a stupid waste of money and manpower. Dolan made a little speech about separating families, calling it a morally reprehensible violation of Catholic principles.

Sheriff Fogarty said, "You should ask the archbishop to intercede. I don't care if they're Commies or not."

I told Fogarty, the Schmitz brothers, and Dolan I would draft a letter for their signatures and have it delivered to their offices. Then I called Archbishop Mitty and explained the situation.

"Tony," he said, "I greatly respect your judgment and I agree with your position in the case. Simple Christian charity means that such matters should never be entrusted to our national government. We must enter a strong objection to the family being separated."

"Besides," he continued, "perhaps there is an opportunity

here. If the family can benefit from our assistance, they may open their hearts and convert to the true faith!"

"Your Excellency," I said, "perhaps beneath your clerical vestments there beats the heart of a lawyer."

There was a second of silence. Then a warm, friendly laugh. "Tony," he said, "all good archbishops revere the newly minted lawyer saint, Thomas More. A model for all clerical statesmen, is he not?"

"I could not agree more, Excellency," I said. "I will deliver a letter to the Chancery Office for your signature."

Next, I dialed MArket 6304, the Labor Council office. I knew the number by heart. Mack Kelly, the president of the organization, was an old friend. He's Irish and I'm Italian, he's from the Mission and I'm from North Beach, but we hit it off from the beginning.

Mack was the first person I called when I returned from my trip to Rome four years ago, after Cardinal Pizzardo gave me his personal approval to organize our Catholic men's group. "Count me in," he said, "And let's get together to plan how to bring my labor guys into this new Catholic crusade. And not just labor, okay? Our whole city needs Catholic Action like this!"

He picked up after two rings. "Tony Bosco," he said cheerfully, "how are you? What can I do for you?" You could still hear a trace of his dad's County Cork accent, tempered by his own boyhood on the mean streets of the Irish working class Mission district.

"Mack, it's good to hear your voice," I said. "I see you still have that 'glad to be alive' enthusiasm despite these dark days we find ourselves in."

"Ah, well, we can't let the bastards get us down," he replied.

"That's exactly why I called. Do you by any chance have a few minutes for me this afternoon? I'd like to tell you about a job I'm doing for Chief O'Reilly — it's on the QT but I know I can trust you to be discreet. And, frankly, I need your help."

"Of course, Tony, come over to the Labor Temple any time after 3:00 and we can meet in my office."

"I'll be there at 3:30," I said.

I came downstairs and found Flora in the kitchen reading the latest *My Day* column by Eleanor Roosevelt. "Listen to this, Tony. It's just what we were talking about last night. She says the fighting in Bataan shows that men from 'different race and background have fought side by side and praise each other's heroism and courage. That lesson should be learned everywhere.' The First Lady would approve of your working with Esther and Larry."

I smiled, walked over to the table and kissed the top of her head. I told her I was going to visit Mack at the Labor Temple, and she asked me to drop her off at her favorite market downtown.

"It's right on the way and I can get a taxi cab back home. It's Monday, and Tony Zanca has tripe on Monday. I'm planning to make you some *Trippa o Busecca alla Milanese* for dinner tonight. You can open us a bottle of that good Dolcetto d'Asti to go with it!"

We put on our coats and hats and went outside. It was one of those early spring mornings when the chilly wind off the Pacific belies the bright sunshine. There was a sharp edge to the fresh smelling air. We both got in the car and I started it up. As we sat waiting for the engine to warm up, I noticed that Flora was wearing her favorite perfume, Shalimar.

We chatted about nothing much as I drove downtown. Before I knew it, I was at the corner of Market and Eighth. The huge Crystal Palace Market was right across the street, dozens of people going in and out. Flora pecked me on the cheek and cheerfully said, "Give my best to Mack, will you?" She got out, gave a little wave, and walked toward the Market. I enjoyed watching her jaunty walk as she crossed the street. It occurred to me we were both in very good spirits today.

I had to work hard to keep up my cheerful disposition as I fought my way through the traffic that clogged the South of Market and Inner Mission districts. White "New Method Laundry" and red "French Laundry" trucks were shuttling back and forth from stifling hot steam-filled commercial laundries in the Mission to hospitals, schools, hotels, and restaurants all over the city.

Mack Kelly, all six feet and five inches of him, gave me a big smile when I walked into his office. He was wearing an expensive looking gray suit and a carnation in his lapel. He sat down in his leather executive chair on a swivel base, with casters that allowed him to roll around, behind his cluttered oak desk. I took the chair in front of the desk. I mentioned how crowded the area seemed between Market and Eighth and Mission and Sixteenth.

"I've never seen this much activity since the last war," he said. "We had that big slump after the war, then the Depression — I remember days when the Inner Mission seemed like a ghost town, even on weekdays! Now you can't get a parking place without going around the block a couple of times. Trucks double-parked everywhere.

"And on Sixth and Howard — remember? — There were guys lined up for two blocks waiting for the free soup at the Salvation Army. Now the only guys you see down there on Skid Row are old winos, too far gone, or too darn lazy, to do anything but panhandle and drink their Gallo rotgut. Anybody who wants a job today can choose between two or three."

Mack always had that Irish "gift of the gab" and I was glad to hear him declaim as usual. With all the terrible changes going on it was comforting to know that some things remained the same.

"Mack," I said, "I can see from the number of guys waiting around downstairs that you're even busier than usual, so I'll get right down to business. I need your help. I can't explain it all to you — maybe someday I will — but I'm working on something sensitive and defense-related for Chief O'Reilly."

"Well," he said, "the chief picked the right guy. Former city supervisor, police commissioner, head of a draft board, and all around Mr. Dependable!" He chortled.

"Thanks, Mack, I always knew you were smartest guy in the room, well, except for yours truly, right? It's good to know your ability to recognize the truth is still A1.

"But seriously," I said, "I need your help to get me, you, Barry Rhodes, and Lewis Geldorf into a room where we can talk frankly and confidentially about a pressing matter involving the city's safety and security. I know that you guys got together with the Chamber of Commerce and set up the Homefront Friends for the Duration, so I thought maybe you would help me with this assignment from the chief."

"You don't ask for much, do you?" Mack said. He rolled back his chair, leaned way back, and crossed his long legs. He looked me in the eye and thought for a moment, then pushed his chair back to the desk, took out a pack of Camels and offered me one. I accepted and he followed suit.

"Those guys don't like us, Tony," Mack said, taking a drag. "They never liked us, since before the big waterfront strike in '34.

Now they like us even less because Harvey London, who used to be Barry Rhodes's pal, has come over to our side. London can't say enough bad stuff about the Commies. He's doing his best to get his sailors into our American Federation of Labor union movement and out of Rhodes's Congress of Industrial Organizations union movement. The same with the seagoing cooks and other shipboard workers."

"Mack, I understand," I said. "And I know Rhodes and Geldorf have another reason to dislike you, me, and London — we're all 'card carrying' Catholics and we've made no bones about how we feel about the Commies and their influence in San Francisco."

"That's a good one," Mack said, laughing. "We go on about how we should beware of 'card carrying communists' but I never heard anybody turn it around like that. Those Christian Brothers over at St. Mary's may not be Jesuits but you've got top notch Jesuitical rhetorical skills!" He leaned so far back in his swivel chair it almost tipped over.

"But maybe my Jesuit education at USF will trump your Christian Brothers brand after all," he said. "You've never met Rhodes or Geldorf before, right?"

"No, never," I said. "But I know that Rhodes doesn't like me. The Commie newspaper quoted him saying that Mayor Rossi and I are 'The Number One Fascist Clown Act in California.'"

Mack raised his eyebrows. "Wow, I missed that. He doesn't pull his punches, Rhodes, I know that, but he's never gotten that personal with me.

"At the same time," he continued, "Rhodes is on the ropes now, because the immigration people are trying to send him back to England. He never became a US citizen. They're accusing him of being a security risk, did you know that?"

"I know," I said, "it's all over the papers for the last several weeks. I think I can see where your Jesuitical cleverness is taking you.

"Are you thinking that Rhodes might want to cultivate all the friendly folks he can get, now that he's being accused, not being the one making the accusations? And since the mayor is my pal, if Rhodes does me a good deed, then I can put in a good word for him with the mayor?"

"Counselor, you are right with me," Mack said. "And since the mayor is a big pal with Mayor LaGuardia in New York City, and since LaGuardia is a big pal of that other New York bigwig President Roosevelt, then Rhodes might think it wouldn't hurt to get on the good side of Mayor Rossi, right? Friends in the right places, and all of that!"

"And of course the Red line is that we are all on the same side for the duration," I added. "According to the paper, Rhodes gave a speech at the university over in Berkeley where he said that all normal politics need to be put on hold so that Americans united can defeat the fascists. Anyway, I don't think he really believes I'm a fascist; he's been using that argument to get at me and the mayor; it's politics, right?"

"Exactly," said Mack. "Well let's give it a try!" He picked up the receiver and dialed a number from memory. I could hear the ring from my side of the desk, then a voice with what sounded like a thick Cockney accent saying, "Hello, this is Barry, who's this?"

"Barry, it's Mack down at the Labor Temple. How are you? Yes, that's good. Well, remember after I helped you sit down with the folks at the Chamber of Commerce, you said you owed me one? Well, I'm calling in my chips. I've got a proposition for you that I think you'll like. Besides, there's a free dinner and drinks involved."

They chatted back and forth like old pals. Mack threw me his pack of Camels and his Zippo, nodding toward them. I lit up and enjoyed a smoke as I listened to Mack's side of the conversation, wondering what Rhodes was thinking after hearing Mack refer to me by name.

After three minutes or so, Mack said, "Okay, you boys are down in the Tenderloin now, right, on Golden Gate Avenue? So we could meet at Branca's on Taylor Street, at 8:30? Excellent. Goodbye, Barry." He put down the receiver and gave me a big smile.

"Okay, Tony, it's all set," he said. "And be sure to bring your checkbook."

"Perfect," I replied, "now let me use your telephone, please. I have to tell Flora not to prepare dinner for tonight."

Chapter 15   Monday, April 13, 1942

Flora was disappointed that we would not be having dinner together, but she told me she would cook the *Trippa* and keep it in the fridge for tomorrow's meal. I had just enough time after calling Flora to stop at my office and compose a letter for General DeWitt, asking him to make an exception allowing Esther to accompany Larry and little Joanie to a detention camp. Bianca, my secretary, typed the letter for me. I folded it, put it in an envelope and slipped it into the inside pocket of my suit coat so I could take it out at dinner.

Tomorrow, I would have one of my bicycle messenger boys take it around to the archbishop, the sheriff, the Assistant U.S. Attorney, and the Schmitz brothers to sign.

I called Dennis and suggested we meet at Bernstein's Fish Grotto on Powell Street for a drink at 7:00. I hadn't seen him since last week. The chief had sent him on a civil defense course at the FBI regional office in Salt Lake City. We had a lot to catch up on before we met the others at Branca's.

I used my permit to park at City Hall again and walked through the Tenderloin. Fifty or so square blocks below Nob Hill between Civic Center and Stockton and Market. Back in Gold Rush times they used to say that if you can't find your favorite debauchery in "the States," just go to San Francisco. These days, they say if you can't find your favorite vice in San Francisco, just go to the Tenderloin.

The sky had clouded up. We could have a shower and I hadn't brought my topcoat. The Tenderloin was crowded with sailors and soldiers. The uniformed servicemen and a seemingly endless procession of other men and women of all sizes, shapes, and descriptions moved in and out of popular watering holes like the bar in the Cadillac Hotel and the Porthole saloon. Civilians, men and women alike, crowded the sidewalks. They wore cheaply made, worn-looking clothes. A surprisingly large number of them were Negroes. They all carried suitcases, cardboard boxes tied up with string, or duffel bags, as they walked to and from the USO, YMCA, YWCA, and other inexpensive hotels in the Tenderloin and the Greyhound Bus Depot on Seventh and Market.

At Powell and Market, I watched the motormen and conductors pushing the cable cars around on the turntable. Raucous young servicemen shouldered each other out of the way to get good seats on the outside of the cars for the trip back up and over Nob Hill to Fisherman's Wharf. I walked a block up the hill to Bernstein's, its gleaming shellacked sailing ship prow façade thrusting out onto the Powell Street sidewalk. Dennis was standing next to the porthole alongside the front door.

"Tony, how are you?" he said with a big smile, his handshake firm and confident. "What a difference between downtown Salt Lake City and here. This place is so alive! Everybody seems to be going somewhere with a purpose, everybody is talking and there's a kind of excitement in the air. It's good to be back home."

"It's good to see you, Dennis," I said. "Let's have a drink and congratulate ourselves on living in San Francisco. I don't know about you, but I doubt whether I could survive in the dour dry capital of the state of Latter Day Saints."

"Well, they did serve 3.5 percent alcohol Near Beer in the restaurants there," Dennis said, "but they sure don't have anything like our Tenderloin!"

We walked into Bernstein's. I smoked a cigarette while we waited for a place at the bar. Once we sat down, we ordered two

Pisco Punches from the bow-tie wearing bartender. I raised my glass to Dennis and said, "Here's to victory."

"To victory," Dennis replied. We clinked glasses and sipped our cocktails.

"What did the FBI teach you at your course?" I asked.

"They spent a lot of time going over basics about policing. What I liked the most was the class on picking locks." He laughed.

"You can show off your new-found knowledge when we check out Harlan Winthrop's residence," I said, laughing back.

"They also made a point of laying down the law to us about how 'loose lips sink ships' and 'He's watching you' and all that malarkey," Dennis said. "They warned us against passing on what they taught us, but I don't think that extends to former police commissioners. I think you should know, for example, about the Bureau's ABC list."

"I know that Hoover has been assembling a list of possibly subversive individuals and organizations since Roosevelt asked him to do it about five years ago," I said. "I don't know the details, but I was under the impression that it includes Germans, Italians, and Japanese people born here as well as immigrants who are legally aliens, right?"

"That's right," Dennis said. "As long as the Bureau decides enough evidence exists to bring a person under suspicion, they are put on the list. The A group has the people who are the first to be arrested — and hundreds of them have been arrested already — and then the B and C group individuals are next. People can be on the list and not be arrested; it all depends on what local agents in charge recommend to Hoover."

"I'm sure I'm on one of those lists," I said. "I've been a citizen since I graduated from college before the First War, but I've been one of the most active people in the city promoting Italian language schools, Columbus Day, and all kinds of other Italian cultural heritage programs. The Italian consulate donated some materials for those after school language classes. I don't know if you remember, but Eddie Sarno's paper claimed that since I was the president of that organization I was promoting fascism. I wouldn't be surprised if some local FBI agent saw that in the paper and added me to the list."

"That could be," Dennis replied. "I got the impression that sometimes they put people on there on the basis of claims made by informants that they pay to go out in the community and dig up dirt. One of the trainers who lectured us put it this way, 'We like to cast a big net and catch all of the fishy characters out there. We'll keep the guilty ones we are looking for, and if we net a few innocent ones? — no harm done, we'll just throw them back in after we check them out.'"

"What a callous point of view," I said. "Think of the shock and fear that innocent people might experience. I'm among the first to demand that we insure the safety and security of our homeland, but there's no need to take such a heartless approach."

"Speaking of being suspects for the government's surveillance, Tony, you said on the phone that we're having dinner with Mack Kelly, Barry Rhodes and Lewis Geldorf. Aren't the immigration people calling for Rhodes to be deported back to England, calling him a threat to national security?"

"Yes," I answered, "I'm counting on his being so angry about the government's behavior that he will want to make common cause with us."

"How do you mean?" Dennis asked.

I told Dennis the whole story about the Yokotas, the Home-front Friends for the Duration organization, about Esther and Larry allegedly knowing of nobody in their Red circles who could have been involved in fifth column work, and how I had promised to try to help their family stay together.

"I'm hoping that Rhodes and Geldorf will cooperate with us, Mack Kelly, and the others — sign our petition to allow the Yokota family to stay together at whatever detention center they are sent to."

"Okay," Dennis said, "and, if I'm following you, you also think you might get them to weigh in about whether they know anybody in their leftist labor network who could have murdered Harlan Winthrop and tried to throw the blame on some Axis supporter or group, right?"

"Yes, Detective," I said, laughing, "exactly! Either that FBI course has sharpened your detecting skills, or working with me has allowed your natural talents to fully bloom!"

"What's all this about blooming?"

I looked over my shoulder and saw Mack Kelly standing behind us. "What are you guys drinking?" he asked. "Don't tell me it's that silly Pisco Punch stuff?

"Bartender!" he shouted, his words easily heard above the chatter, "Bring me a pint of Rainier Old Stock."

"Yes, sir, Mr. Kelly, coming right up," the bartender replied.

He made a disappointed face. "How you allegedly intelligent men can sit and drink those girlie concoctions when you could be drinking beer brewed in one of our very own San Francisco establishments I will never understand."

"Hello, Mack," I said. "Do you know Detective Sullivan?

Dennis, this is Mack Kelly." Dennis turned and shook hands with Mack.

"Mr. Kelly," he said, "it's a great pleasure to meet a fellow Don. As far as I can see, those Jesuits at USF law school did nothing to stunt your growth, that's for sure."

"It's my pleasure, Detective," said Mack, "and call me Mack, will ya? By the time I went to USF, I had survived Sacred Heart High School, hurricanes and typhoons at sea, and the temptations of countless Manila waterfront dives. I had, as it were, lots of immunity against black robed practitioners of Catholic casuistry."

"I wonder what kind of casuistry we're going to get from Rhodes and Geldorf?" Dennis said.

"Well, they're communists, not Catholics," I said. "Don't you think we're more likely to get *The Communist Manifesto*, not *The Summa Theologica*? Marx and Engels, not Thomas Aquinas? Stalin, not Pius XII?"

"Tony's always had his head in the clouds," Mack said. "Ever since he was a kid winning all those scholarship medals at Sacred Heart and St. Mary's."

"I'd put my money on Rhodes and Geldorf being practical union men looking to make deals benefiting their men, not moralistic politicians trying to make laws suiting their God, like Tony here."

I rolled my eyes. "What Mack ignores, Dennis, is that because they're communists, they'll want to make a deal that serves their interest as they define it according to their Red Theology. We can't forget that what makes the whole Red movement so strong is that it offers people a religion to believe in and a faith to practice — it's just not the Christian religion."

I hoped Dennis wasn't getting tired of my lectures, but I couldn't resist. "They certainly do have a theology — you can buy the books that contain their dogma at the International Book Store on McAllister Street, for heaven's sake! And where we have priests to interpret the theology for the people, they have commissars!"

"The way I see it, you're both right," Dennis said. "I'd put it this way — Commies and Catholics are being practical and making deals all the time, but not all Catholics or all Commies care about the fine points of their respective theologies. But look at the time!" He held up his arm and showed his Gruen Curvex wristwatch. "We only have a few blocks to go, but we better get going or we'll be late for our meeting."

We paid for our drinks and pushed our way through the customers lined up three-deep at the bar to make our way outside to Powell, where we were greeted by the loud clang and the metallic clatter of a cable car passing us on the way to the top of Nob Hill.

It must have rained while we were in Bernstein's; the tires of cars going by made a squishing sound on the street. The neon signs above the Pig'n Whistle Restaurant and The Owl Drug Company reflected off the glistening wet streets. I gave nickels to a couple of wet and miserable looking old men huddled in the doorway of A.P. Giannini's new Bank of America headquarters at the corner of Powell and Eddy.

The crowds on Eddy as we walked uptown to Taylor Street made it impossible to talk, but we made it in five minutes, right on time. Tony Salardino came up to us as we pushed past the curtain inside the front door. Directly in front of us on the right was a counter with a dozen seats. To the left were a dozen tables. I hadn't realized that Salardino had gotten such a small place.

"Commissioner Bosco, welcome to Branca's," Salardino said. "I don't think you've graced us with your company in this new place, right?"

"That's right," I replied, "and let me introduce my companions, Mack Kelly and Dennis Sullivan."

"I'm very pleased to welcome you all to Branca's," said Salardino.

Just then, several people came through the curtain and stood right behind us. I recognized Barry Rhodes and Lewis Geldorf from their pictures in *The Examiner*, *The Chronicle*, *The News*, and *The Call-Bulletin*. Ever since the Big Strike in '34, scarcely a month went by without an article or two about the dockworkers and their leaders.

They both wore double-breasted suits, white shirts, and ties. Rhodes had a narrow face with a distinctive large nose that hooked down at the end. Geldorf was movie-star handsome, with a more oval face and well-proportioned features. They both combed their hair straight back, but Rhodes's brown hair was thinning and Geldorf's black hair was thick.

They appeared to have come in accompanied by a woman, but I didn't recognize her. She was very attractive, about the same age as Ruthie, with red hair, freckles, a pale complexion, and bright blue eyes.

I made introductions all around as Tony Salardino moved several tables together to make room for all of us. Much to my surprise, Rhodes introduced the young woman as Barbara O'Connell Bates, Ruthie's friend.

We all gave our hats to Salardino, and Bates gave him her coat. None of us had brought topcoats.

When we finally sat down around three square tables pushed together, there was a moment of awkward silence.

Finally, Rhodes spoke. "Well, gentlemen," he said in a nasally voice I thought came out of either the East London docklands or the mill district of Birmingham, "this is the first time we lowly tribunes of the working people have received an invitation to meet and dine with California's Catholic Capitalist Labor Aristocracy! To what noble cause shall we attribute this great honor?"

"Mr. Rhodes," I replied, "I would like to thank you and your colleague for agreeing to meet. I'll be blunt." I looked him in the eye. "We need your help to resolve an issue that could well affect our safety and security here in San Francisco right now, as we cope with the challenges of this war. It is a war that none of us wanted to fight, but it requires our united action if we are to persist and win."

Rhodes lit a cigarette and looked thoughtful.

"I can't resist asking about your accent," I said. "Is it East London, or Birmingham? I've been to both places and know it's hard to tell those two accents apart."

"Ah, Commissioner, your ears deceive you," he replied. "It's neither East London nor Birmingham. I grew up in the West End of London."

"I already knew that," Mack Kelly said. "Barry and I went to sea as young lads because we wanted adventure, but my dad was more of a 'horny handed son of toil' than his. Right, Barry?"

"Yeah, course that's true. My people are bankers and real estate brokers. My pa wasn't loading and unloading boats in the Thames the way Mack's dad was doing here on Frisco Bay. In fact, I've been thinking lately, if they deport me back home the way they want to, I can get a job selling real estate. Though with all those bombs the fascists have been dropping, who'd want to buy a house in London, eh?"

"So you're not somebody who rose up out of the working class to lead your people to a more just and equitable society?" Dennis asked.

"Well, yes and no. Look at it this way. Mack and I saw with our own eyes the evils of the wage labor system in the years we worked aboard ship. We decided we had to get rid of that wage slavery and create a better future for our fellow workers."

"Right," Mack jumped in, "Barry and I want the same thing. We work for our members, and if our members do well, the city will do well. Isn't that right, Barry?"

"Absolutely," Barry replied. "We might have some differences, sure. But neither of us goes around making speeches about Marx and Engles or Popes Leo and Pius."

Barbara O'Connell Bates had put up her hand and was waving it around. "It's hard to get a word in if you're just a girl, *gentlemen,* but I have something different that I'd like to say."

All of us men at the table uttered guilty grunts of assent and words of encouragement.

"Along with Lewis here," she said, "I had my eyes opened while I was a student at Berkeley. It was clear to me that the Communist Party was the only organization with a scientific understanding of history. The party had a willingness to actually fight to help move history in the positive direction for humanity. I'm a communist and I'm proud of it!"

"Barbara," Lewis said, "you shouldn't presume to speak for me. I was attracted to the Party when we were students, but my allegiance is to my country, and of course to our people in the union. The way I see it, I'm a practical man who spends his days — and sometimes nights — looking for ways to serve my men and their families."

This is my cue, I thought, but I said, "Let's order some food and drink and then continue our discussion."

I called Harry Chezzi over. Harry looked professional in his white jacket and shirt and black bow tie. We all gave him our orders. I asked everyone if they would like a couple of bottles of Branca's best Chianti. They agreed and Harry hurried off to put in our orders.

"Now, speaking of being practical," I said, "I want to go back to the reason I asked you all to be here. When I asked Mack if he thought you two gentlemen would sit down with me, he was skeptical."

"We all know that you folks from the dockworkers don't always see eye to eye with this city government," Mack explained, "and of course Tony has been an unofficial adviser to the mayor from the beginning."

"Nevertheless," I said, "it seemed to me that we are all on the same side now — we have one single goal, and that is to do whatever is necessary to defeat the Axis. That means we also want to make sure nothing, and I mean nothing, interferes with our morale here in San Francisco."

Dennis chimed in. "Tony and I are working with Chief O'Reilly to stop a threat to our Homefront morale." He turned to me.

"Be frank," I said. "We want to hear anything you might know about a fifth column operating on the Left here in the City. Anything you can share with us would be important. We can't tell you the details now; maybe sometime in the future when this threat is neutralized, but right now we ask you to trust us and help us out."

The waiter brought our meals. Five of us asked for the daily special — braised rabbit with polenta and greens. Barbara ordered a broiled rib steak, on the rare side, with mashed potatoes. Harry opened the two bottles Chianti Classico, poured us each a glass and wished us, *"Buon Appetito."*

As we ate, Rhodes said, "Commissioner, I will be frank with you. I've always said that Angelo Rossi and you were fascists. I said that to reporters and anybody who would listen. But here we are having a good meal, safe and secure, while Nazi bombs are killing civilians in Europe and England and Tojo's troops are beheading innocent people in Asia. But listen here, I never believed you and Rossi were actual fascists.

"And I want to help anyway I can to keep our morale high and defeat the Axis powers. I think that goes for Lewis and Barbara, too."

They both nodded.

"Barry and I have already made a half dozen speeches calling for unity for victory," Geldorf said.

Bates said, "The Party education curriculum is one hundred percent focused on the need for Homefront unity and all-out effort to defeat the Axis."

"Have any of the three of you heard any talk, even gossip, about any underground organization trying to weaken morale?" Dennis asked.

"We're dead set against such activities," Rhodes said.

"Can we all keep in touch, so that if any such information like this comes up, you can let us know?" I asked, and they all agreed.

The waiter was clearing away our dishes when Harry Chezzi returned to the table and asked if any of us wanted dessert. When we all passed he said, "I will bring over our best Grappa for you all — it's on the house."

While we all took a sip of our brandy, I pulled out the letter to General DeWitt.

I smiled. "Now that we have pledged ourselves to each other as allies, at least for the duration, and having broken bread together, I have a favor to ask."

I opened the letter, held it up for everyone to see, and explained the dilemma Esther, Larry and Joanie found themselves in. I asked them if they would sign it so it could be delivered to the general tomorrow.

Barbara was clearly surprised to hear me advocating on behalf of the Yokota family. "How do you know the Yokotas?" she asked.

"Ruthie Fuller is working with us," I said

"Ruthie?" Barbara asked. "She's a friend of mine. Of course I'll sign the letter."

After everyone signed, I folded it and replaced it in the envelope. We toasted to victory, finished our Grappa, shook hands, and left the restaurant.

Chapter 16   Tuesday, April 14, 1942

A terrifying loud roaring sound woke me up as the house vibrated. I jumped out of bed in my pajamas and got to the window just in time to see five bright blue planes flying in tight formation over the Golden Gate Bridge, heading toward the Farallon Islands. The sun was up and the sky was clear. I watched as they flew out to sea, then turned back when they reached the Farallones. Flora, tying her bathrobe, joined me at the window just in time to see the planes flying right across from us over the Marina before heading toward the East Bay.

"Tony!" she cried. "They are flying so low! What kind of planes are those?"

"They can't be flying much above one thousand feet, given how close they came to the tops of the bridge towers," I answered. "They look like the Navy's new torpedo bombers called Avengers. Those young pilots over at the Alameda Naval Air Station are showing off by flying so low over the bridge."

"They're called Avengers?" she asked. "They're beautiful planes! Did you see how they are painted light blue on the bottom and darker blue on top?"

"Yes, that's for camouflage," I explained. "They're beautiful all right, and powerful, too. Just imagine, our Buick Century can produce 165 horsepower. Those Grumman Avengers can produce up to 1700. I've read that they're a lot more powerful than the Jap planes that bombed Pearl Harbor."

As the sound of the Avengers faded off in the distance, Flora said, "Tony, I've been meaning to talk to you about something."

"What is it?" I asked. "If it's about my missing dinner, I'm sorry and I can explain."

"No, not at all. I know how busy you are with your work for the chief. Anyway, I'm just going to serve yesterday's dinner today. It's still fresh and perfectly good in the fridge.

"This is a completely different thing, and I hope you won't be offended, but whenever you talk about the Japanese, you say 'Jap' and I can't help but cringe every time you do that."

I sighed and remembered Ruthie complaining about my saying "Commies."

Flora is good at reading my expressions. She noticed me hesitating, and said, "Yesterday afternoon, after I took the groceries home, I went to a meeting of my Conference of Christians and Jews organization. It was at the Women's City Club."

"That's Jake Oster's outfit," I said. "He's always asking me to participate but I'm so busy in so many other activities already."

"You make it sound like its Jake's private club or something," she retorted. "Jake is the president, but actually it seems like more women come to the meetings than men.

"Anyway, your friend Harold McKinnon gave a wonderful talk about what he called 'The Internal Threats' to our liberties as we fight to keep our freedoms."

"Harold's a fine speaker," I said. "We recently elected him to be the president of our new St. Thomas More Society of Catholic lawyers."

"Well," Flora said, "one of his points was that we need to treat all of our fellow Americans with dignity and respect. We're all children of the same God.

"He insisted that we need to show respect for all people. It doesn't matter whether they came from Europe like we did, or from China, or Japan, or Africa for that matter.

"One of the ladies asked if he thought it was all right to use words like 'Jap' and 'Chink' and he said he thought it was very disrespectful. A bunch of us were talking after his lecture. We had a big argument about what to do. We couldn't all agree."

"So, what are you saying?"

"I was thinking about it last night before you came home. Remember how rude the manager at the Hotel Coronado was to us on our honeymoon? We were so upset we walked right out."

"Oh, I know what you are thinking of. He told the bell boy 'take these Wop suitcases up to room 303.'"

"Yes, see how you remember it so clearly? You can recall it word for word even after all these years."

"I'm sure you are right, Flora," I said. "It's interesting that Ruthie Fuller pointed out the same thing when I called her friends Esther and Larry 'Commies.'"

I chuckled. "It looks like I have two strikes against me. I better be careful or I'll be struck out!"

"I'm relieved that you are being a good sport about this," Flora said. "You know I don't like to criticize you."

"Flora, you know that I *want* you to be my number one critic! I'm lucky you're here to remind me of the Golden Rule."

Flora smiled. "I know, Tony, but sometimes I find myself acting more like my mother than myself."

"Well, *most of the time*," I chuckled, "you don't have any trouble being a good critic."

"Speaking of critics and the Golden Rule," I added, "the mayor and Mack Kelly were both talking about something like this last month. The Municipal Railway hired a young Negro man, but when he went to work the streetcar men refused to work with him."

"Oh, that's right!" Flora said, "When he and his wife came to dinner a couple of weeks ago Mack was going on about 'all men are created equal,' especially now because we are fighting to preserve our rights!"

"Yes, exactly. And you know, speaking of Negroes, I was noticing yesterday when I was down in the Tenderloin — I must have seen dozens of Negro people!"

"I noticed a lot of them at the Crystal Palace Market, too," Flora said. "And when I took the streetcar down Fillmore Street the other day, it seemed like lots more Negro people were getting off and on at the stops from California Street all the way down to McAllister."

"They're here looking for work," I explained. "Heaven knows, with so many men already gone to fight we'll need thousands of new workers doing the loading and unloading at Fort Mason and the Embarcadero."

I told her about all the activity I'd seen driving to the Labor Temple, at the warehouses, factories, and construction sites.

"Speaking of work," I said, "I'd better shower and shave and get ready to meet Dennis and Ruthie. We are supposed to report to the chief at 9:00 sharp."

"I'll go downstairs and prepare us some breakfast," Flora said.

She made some French brioche to go with our cappuccino. I

preferred biscotti, but I had to admit it complemented the coffee very well. I was thinking that I hadn't seen Jake Oster since the last meeting of the mayor's civil defense committee two weeks after Pearl Harbor.

"Did Jake preside at your meeting?" I asked Flora. "He must be in his seventies now. It's impressive that he stays so active after all these years."

"Yes, he did," Flora said. "He gave a nice introduction to Mr. McKinnon. He made everyone laugh when he said he was glad to have a famous Catholic legal scholar as the speaker and so many Catholics in the audience."

"Everybody laughed because they know that the archbishop has been standoffish about this organization. He doesn't want to forbid us from joining it, because he believes in human brother-hood, but he doesn't want to encourage us to join it either, be-cause it's not a Catholic organization."

"I always have a hard time addressing Jake by his first name," Flora said. "I said, 'Hello, Mr. Oster' and he laughed and said, 'Isn't it about time after all these years that you call me Jake'?"

"Well it's only natural that you would still call him Mr. Os-ter," I said. "After all, you first met him when you were still just a high school girl visiting Linette, at their house. Old habits die hard, right?"

"Yes," she said. "And speaking of Linette, we are going to-gether to the Palace Hotel this afternoon."

"We should invite Jake and Mildred to dinner again. After all, we've been family ever since your cousin married Linette all those years ago."

"That's a great idea, Tony."

"What's on today?" I asked, "Are you ladies having lunch at the Palace Court Restaurant?"

"No, Tony," Flora replied. "You make it sound like all I do is sit around with other ladies and drink tea and eat cookies!

"Actually, the National Conference of Catholic Women is having its West Coast Convention at the Palace Hotel. Linette and I are the chairwomen of the Race Relations Committee."

"It's no wonder you are sensitive about the importance of using respectful language," I said.

"That's right. And our committee is proposing a resolution at today's meeting. In fact, can you listen to it and tell me if you think it's written well?"

"Of course!"

I poured myself another cup of cappuccino and waited for her to return.

Flora returned with a typewritten page in her hand. "Okay, what do you think of this?"

She read from the paper. "Racial prejudice and hatred is contrary both to Catholic teaching and to American principles. We must defeat the totalitarian States, which are the foremost proponents of the false and contemptible doctrine of racial inequality."

"That's excellent," I said. "You need to put it into what I call 'resolution language' but otherwise I think it's exactly the sort of reminder about the principles we live by and that we are fighting for that we need today. *Brava, mia moglie, Ti amo!*"

"*Grazie, mio marito, Anch' io ti amo!* But if you're going to meet your *compagni* at the Hall of Justice at 9:00, you'd better get going, *Subito!*"

Chapter 17   Tuesday, April 14, 1942

avoided the Marina and the traffic around Fort Mason by taking Union Street over Russian Hill. At the top I could see Treasure Island in the distance. According to *The Chronicle,* the Navy laid down the law telling Mayor Rossi that it was taking over the island tomorrow. That kind of high-handed exercise of tyrannical national power is unacceptable. Jake Oster, for one, would surely agree.

Jake Oster — I thought back to when I first met him. It must have been during the hunt for the people who bombed the parade at the foot of Market Street back in '16.

I stopped at my office, gave the letter for General DeWitt to Bianca, and asked her to have a messenger boy take it around for signatures and then hand-deliver it to Fort Mason.

At the Portsmouth Square Garage, Charlie O'Brian told me their business was going up so much he'd had to hire two helpers. Ruthie and Dennis were waiting for me in the lobby of the Hall of Justice. Ruthie was dressed all in navy blue today; I thought it suited her. If she was still upset about her cousin Patrick, it didn't show on her face. Dennis had on a decidedly new gray chalk-striped suit with a maroon handkerchief in the breast pocket that matched his tie and complemented his dark eyes and hair.

It was a few minutes after 9:00. Maggie looked exhausted, her eyes bloodshot. "Good morning, you three," she said. "I hope you get a better reception than I did a half hour ago. He's been working ten to twelve hour days, and guess who has been working overtime to help him," she complained. "He's determined to make sure that everything is properly organized for the big raid the department is doing with the FBI and the Army.

It's not scheduled to take place until the 21st, a week from now, but you'd think it was tomorrow, the way he's been acting."

"I'm not on the commission any more but I know about this," I said. "All the Bay Area police and sheriff's departments will fan out and blanket the whole six counties, along with agents from the FBI and soldiers from the Army. They're making sure they have arrested any Japanese who haven't registered for the detention centers."

"They're also targeting the people on Hoover's ABC list that I mentioned," Dennis said to me. He turned to Ruthie. "This is a list of potentially dangerous people that President Roosevelt ordered the FBI to draw up way back before Pearl Harbor."

"Oh no," Ruthie said. "Will they be going after Larry?"

"Larry already registered," I said. "In fact he even attempted to enlist in the Army but they won't allow him to join up because he's what they call a Kibei — born in the USA but educated in Japan. Speaking of which, I'm having a letter delivered to the general this morning asking for an exception to allow Esther and little Joanie to go to the detention center."

"That's wonderful news," Ruthie said. "Have you told Esther and Larry?"

"No, but maybe you can telephone them after we meet with the chief, okay?"

"Sure, and thank you, Tony," Ruthie said.

The chief opened his door and ushered us in.

He looked even worse than he did the last time we met. "What do you have to report?" he asked in a tired voice. "Did you have any better luck tracing the murder to the Commies than you did tracing it to those crazy Catholic Mexicans?"

"Chief, I'll be honest," I said, "we are kind of stalemated. Unless we get some new leads, we are no closer to finding the killer today than we were a week ago.

"We still haven't made contact with anybody in those Red groups who won't support the war. There aren't many of them and I doubt whether they would go so far as murder Winthrop and leave that pro-Axis graffiti, but I'd like to eliminate them from suspicion. Beyond that, I don't know that there's much more we can do."

"Tony, I've been thinking," Ruthie said. "I should spend some time with my friends at the School of Fine Arts who are Left-wingers like that. They're Trotskyites and they hate the Communist Party. Some belong to the Socialist Workers Party, some to that Young People's Socialist League. Some don't belong to anything, but they always go to marches and stuff.

"I mean I can't go around asking them questions but, you know, I can invite them to my apartment in North Beach, or go to their studios in the Montgomery Block. We can drink wine and I can keep my ears open."

The chief shook his head, with a weary expression. "All these different Red outfits — it makes me tired just thinking about it."

"That's a great idea, Ruthie," Dennis said. "Maybe the chief here can give you some money for the wine." He chuckled.

"Dammit, detective, this is no laughing matter," O'Reilly shouted, turning into his old self again. "Tony, I gave you an assignment. So far I've got nothing to show for it but Dennis's lousy joke and your bum story about wanting to do favors for some mixed race Commie couple, one of whom is a Jap to boot.

"What about Coit Tower? Has Major Brody cleaned everything up and reopened it to the public?"

"That's all taken care of, chief," I answered. "He assured me that there's not a trace of that RoBerTo sign on the wall. He's been open for business for a week now."

"And what are we going to do about Harlan Winthrop?" the chief continued. "Dennis, have you gotten any inquiries from his family down in the detective bureau? Calls from family members wondering what happened to him?"

"Winthrop was a bachelor," Dennis said. "I checked all the usual records. He doesn't seem to have had any family here."

"Dennis is right about that," I added. "I knew him for years and know that he came out here as a young man and went into a banking and shipping business owned by one of his relatives in the East. He was active in the Chamber of Commerce, but he didn't seem to have much of a social life. Flora and I never saw him at the Opera or the Symphony.

"The one social event that I remember he regularly attended was the beginning of the yachting season down at the St. Francis Yacht Harbor. Flora and I always go with my cousin Carlo. Carlo has a boat down there and we never miss the big Opening Day on the Bay party. Carlo has a big sailboat, but Harlan was always at the helm of a good-looking cabin cruiser with his banker friends, all drinking Champagne and having a good time."

"We still need to check out Harlan Winthrop's residence," Dennis said.

"What? You still haven't done that?" Chief O'Reilly blurted out.

"Chief," I said, "we followed up on our theories about the RoBerTo sign first. Since this is not an ordinary homicide case and we're keeping it quiet, I didn't see any reason to go to Winthrop's apartment right away. But I haven't just neglected the job."

"Do you know where he lived?" Ruthie asked.

"Sure," Dennis said. "Tony had me look it up. He had a place in the Chambord Apartments on Nob Hill."

"That's on Sacramento Street behind Grace Episcopal Cathedral," I said.

"We'll need a search warrant for that," O'Reilly said.

"Not really," Dennis replied. "First of all, that would mean we'd have to include a judge in this investigation, and we sure don't want to do that. Secondly, one of the little benefits I received from my FBI course in Salt Lake City is this dandy little helper." He pulled what looked like a small leather wallet from his pants pocket.

"They even had us practice using it," he said, showing us a set of lock picks he took out of the wallet. "I can even pick a lock in the dark, if you don't mind me saying so."

"Well, I'm glad to see you're going to make good use of that FBI course," O'Reilly said.

"How about his church activities?" Ruthie asked, "Should we be checking with his pastor and see if members of his congregation have been asking about him at Mass?"

"Actually," I said, "Harlan was not Catholic. I know for a fact that he had no use for religion and didn't belong to a church. He made a big point of that in public. It was after I helped Archbishop Hanna organize that mass march down Market Street. The protest march that the Knights of Columbus held to protest the Klan."

"I remember that," O'Reilly said. "That was in '24, so you youngsters weren't there, but tens of thousands of Catholics were out there demonstrating against the KKK. I marched in the big police department contingent."

"Right," I said. "Well, I was at a smoker after a Chamber of Commerce event a week or so after that march. After he probably had one too many bourbons, Harlan declared that it was pointless to demonstrate against the KKK. He said that evolution favors the White Anglo Saxon race. The Irish and Italians and all other lesser races are bound to go extinct like the dinosaurs."

"I bet he supported Senator Phelan's 'Keep California White' campaign back in 1920," Dennis said.

"Oh, he was on the committee that raised money for Phelan," I said. "He claimed that religion was just superstition, a plot by the weak to interfere with the freedom of the strong. I remember his words clearly. He said, 'All of your religious claptrap about the meek shall inherit the Earth is nonsense. The strong are meant by nature to dominate, and the White Anglo Saxon race is the strongest of the strong. All the inferior races will go into the dustbin of history.'"

"What did you say?" Ruthie asked. "That sounds like he *belonged to* the KKK!"

"Well, you know, at an occasion like that where somebody drinks too much and starts making outlandish speeches, people tend to just ignore them and walk away. As I recall, nobody said anything. We all just moved on to talk to other guests."

"Hmm," said the Chief, "after hearing that, just between us here, I have less sympathy for him than I did before. Still, we need to find out who killed him and bring him to justice.

"Tony, let's make some progress in this case. If necessary, I can see to it that Winthrop is quietly cremated and his ashes scattered in the Bay, but I'd rather we get to the bottom of this."

"That seems callous. What if somebody calls the department asking about him?" Ruthie asked.

"If that happens we'll open a missing person file," the chief replied. "Then the file will get lost. If anybody ever learns about this case, it will become just another of hundreds of unsolved missing person cases. We have to be practical. Above all, dammit, we need to make sure the public's not riled up about some fifth column work."

"We'd better make sure that none of the papers ever get wind of the murder," I said. "We'll just have to trust that everyone we've talked to, and Brody, and anybody in the department who heard about it, will keep it quiet."

We left the chief, said goodbye to Maggie, and walked over to Fosters, where we sat down with our coffee and donuts and talked about what to do next.

"I'll call the Yokotas and let them know you sent that letter to General DeWitt," Ruthie said.

"Good," I said. "Dennis, let's check out Winthrop's apartment and his boat." I smiled at him. "I think our ethics teachers at St. Mary's College might object, but Harlan is dead. He's not worried about somebody violating his privacy and besides, there's a war on."

Chapter 18   Tuesday, April 14, 1942

ennis and Ruthie went off on their respective chores, and I decided to see for myself what kind of job Major Brody had done in cleaning up the "Library" mural at Coit Tower. The place was crawling with soldiers and sailors and other visitors in civilian clothes. Neither the wall nor the floor showed any sign of the murder.

At lunch, there were more reminders of how the war was transforming the city. I was hungry by the time I started walking back down the hill to my office so I stopped at Nick Finocchio's New Tivoli for lunch. Nick told me that he hired two new waiters. "Neither one of them speak a word of Italian, but so what — none of these new customers speak Italian either. These young servicemen drink so much wine, I had to double my last order."

I walked down Grant Avenue and took Columbus to my office on Montgomery, where I spent the rest of the afternoon catching up on my work for the Italian consulate. Now that we're at war with Italy, it's much more difficult to settle these inheritance claims for Italian citizens living in the old country who are the designated heirs of relatives over here. It took me and Bianca all afternoon to prepare and then get ready to mail only five claims.

It was almost 7:00 when I picked up my car from Charlie. The traffic was bad, even using Union Street to go back to Pacific Heights. When I got home I saw that somebody had parked a brand new Cadillac convertible in my usual spot in front of the house.

The house felt different. Even if I hadn't seen the car outside, something in the air alerted me to the fact that we had a visitor.

"Tony," I heard Flora say, "we're here in the kitchen."

She was sitting at the kitchen table with Linette Bassano, her Cousin Alex's wife, Jake Oster's daughter. There was a tea pot and two empty cups on the table. I've always liked Linette, and she's become a classic beauty now that she's in her late forties. Today, her striking green eyes were bloodshot, and her face appeared swollen from crying. Flora looked worried.

"Hello, Flora, Hello, Linette," I said. "Flora told me you were both attending the NCCW meeting at the Palace Hotel, but I didn't know we would have the pleasure of your company today. You both look upset. What has happened?"

They looked at each other for several seconds before Flora said, "Tony, Linette wanted to talk to you about something that has burdened her for the past two weeks. She feels like she needs your help."

"Well, of course, I'm happy to help in any way I can. What's troubling you?"

"This is a family matter, Tony. I'm not supposed to tell anyone about it," she said, "but I can't keep it inside me any longer. I would tell my confessor, but it's something to do with the law. You used to be a police commissioner, and you've helped my father with so many sensitive legal problems for so many years..." Her voice broke before she could finish her thought. She was twisting a napkin in her hands as she spoke.

I sat beside her. "Well, sometimes it helps to just start at the beginning," I said.

"But my father swore us all to silence," she explained. "I feel like I'm betraying him if I say anything. I just don't know what to do, or who to turn to."

"Sometimes we have to trust our instincts and follow our conscience," I answered. "I'm sure that Jake would want you to do that."

"And, anyway," Flora said, "Tony and I will keep this confidential."

"Of course," I said.

"I was all right keeping this to myself until the middle of the discussion about our race relations resolution today. But something about the whole question of justice and doing the right thing just sort of made me choke up. I just couldn't stop myself."

"Excuse me for a second," I said. I walked into the dining room, took our bottle of Vecchia Romagna brandy out of the liquor cabinet and poured each of us a drink. "Let's make this easier; take a sip of this, Linette, and then start at the beginning."

Linette obliged. "It all started when Louie Chen, our family cook for over twenty years, told my dad he needed help because a terrible thing had happened."

Chapter 19 Wednesday, April 15, 1942

found myself thinking about Linette's story when I woke up this morning. Flora and I needed to arrange to meet with the Osters.

Then I stepped outside to pick up my newspaper and started thinking about Eddie Sarno. His *Il Corriere del Popolo* was there on the doorstep along with *The San Francisco Chronicle.*

Taking a look at the headlines, I decided that the first order of business today should be to do something that had been at the back of my mind since I met Ruthie at The Riviera on Sunday.

I went upstairs to my study and made two telephone calls. The first one was to Mack Kelly, who gave me the private telephone number for Barry Rhodes. Then I called Barry.

"Tony," he said, "how can I be of service to my new fellow ally in the Great Patriotic War, as they call it back in Mother Russia?" I could hear the barely suppressed laughter in his voice from the way he exaggerated his West End accent.

"First, Barry, I'd like to thank you for meeting with Mack, Dennis and me," I said. "I want you to know how much I appreciate your assuring us that we can count on your help."

"Well, course, counselor," he replied, "we can't be lettin any old resentments interfere with our achieving victory against fascist aggression."

"I agree one hundred percent," I said. "Actually, that's the second thing I called you about. Eddie Sarno is still using his paper to stoke the old rivalries in our Italian community. He's keeping alive divisions that are hurting our war effort. In today's issue, his headline reads 'Mayor Rossi and his Fascist Friend Bosco Raise Thousands of Dollars for Mussolini.'"

I could hear him lighting one of his ever-present cigarettes and taking a drag. "Is there any truth to it?" he asked.

"Of course not," I replied sharply. "The article is about how our local branch of the Italian Catholic *Caritas* is sending money through the Red Cross for Italian widows and orphans. These are innocent women and children. None of the money goes to the fascist regime. None."

"Well, I got no beef with the Red Cross," Barry said. "The boys in our union raised money for Red Cross ambulances that went to Spain to help in the war against fascism there."

"We were on different sides on that one, I admit, but we're on the same side now. I know this is asking a lot, but is there any way you could lean on Eddie Sarno a little, or have somebody you know lean on him? Ask him to lay off me and the mayor? Like you said at dinner, you know that we have never really supported the fascists.

"I think Eddie knows it, too, but he's like a dog with a bone. For whatever reasons, and my wife thinks it's personal with him, he just can't stop lashing out at what he calls *the prominenti,* the business and professional guys who still support the Church. Me, especially. It would mean a lot to our Italian community if Eddie quit stirring up our people. We need to be united to win this 'Great Patriotic War.'"

"You lawyers — you sure know how to make a good argument," Barry said. "I have some friends in the newspaper business. I'll give Sarno a call and spread the word to my friends that he needs to quiet down and stop attacking you 'Good Italian Catholics.'" He did his exaggerated London accent again. "I expect you won't see any more of these attacks in his paper."

I thanked him and told him to be sure to let me know if I could do anything for him in the future.

"Well, counselor," he said, "I seem to be in need of good lawyering these days. You might hear from me soon, though I hope not." He laughed. "Maybe they'll get tired of trying to throw me out of the country, but you never know."

We said goodbye and I hung up the telephone. It would be a great relief to be rid of Eddie Sarno's vitriolic diatribes.

Flora called up that breakfast was ready. "After last night, I decided we needed to begin the day with something sweet," she said, "so I made us a *sfogliate* with apricots that I canned last year when we had that especially good crop."

"How wonderful!" I said, "You know how much I love apricots. I was thinking when I woke up today that we have so many things to be grateful for. One of them is our farm in Los Altos. This war won't last forever, and one of the things I look forward to is spending more time there. Not just the odd weekend, but longer stretches — having friends over and entertaining our family."

"That's a nice thought," she agreed. She poured us each a cup of Caffe latte and sat down across from me.

"I was thinking I should call Jake Oster this morning," I said. "We need to hear what their cook has to say so we can understand what is going on."

"I agree," Flora said. "We can't really do anything until we know the whole story."

"Well, yes, and also — in cases like this it often happens that the people caught up in an event have different versions of what happened, because they saw the event from different points of view."

"Right. I understand. Remember rehearsing arguments with me before a trial? I've said you'd make a different argument if you were for the defendant rather than the plaintiff!"

"You're right on both counts, counselor," I said. "I *have* been annoyed, but it's also true that from the judge's point of view it's important to see as many sides to the matter as possible."

Flora laughed. "I'll never forget that time we invited young Joe Monahan and his wife to dinner, when you and he and John Dolan, I think it was…"

"I remember that dinner," I said. "We were celebrating John's becoming Assistant U.S. Attorney for this region. We all raved about your *coniglio in umido con peperoni e cipolle,* if I remember correctly. Which of course, *carissima moglie,* brings up another conundrum, which is that our memories play tricks on us. So seeing the whole picture is sometimes very difficult, *non e vero?*"

"Sometimes just finishing my story is very difficult, *Commis-sioner,*" Flora said, rolling her eyes. "I was remembering — okay? — Yes, remembering! You said there is always more than one side to a question. And Joe said, 'I agree completely, there's my side and the wrong side.'"

We both laughed. I reached across the table, took her right hand in both of my hands and kissed it. "I love you darling." I walked over to the stove. "Shall I pour us some more Caffe latte?"

Flora got up from the table as well and started to collect the plates. "No thanks, Tony, but let's call Jake Oster and make an appointment to visit the Oster family."

"Yes, and I can't really be of service until we get the whole story."

I went back upstairs to my study. It was early enough in the day that Jake could still be at home. I had his home telephone number from when we wrote an article for the state Chamber of Commerce magazine almost ten years ago. We both argued the National Industrial Recovery Act was a good law, me from a Democratic Party point of view, him from a Republican Party point of view.

I dialed TUxedo 1516 and listened to it ring three times, then a deep voice said, "Hello, this is Jake Oster."

"Jake, it's Tony Bosco."

"Good morning, Tony, I was expecting a call from you. Linette called me last night and said you wanted to talk about something very important, but she didn't say what it was."

"Well," I replied, "Flora saw Linette yesterday and we were thinking it's been a long time since we saw you. Can we get together with your wife and Linette?"

"I'm betting it's something about the resolution on race relations they presented at yesterday's meeting of their Catholic Women's Conference. Linette was upset when so many people objected that it was much too outspoken. She told me how the group voted to table the resolution and called for it to be revised and reconsidered at the next meeting, I thought she was close to tears."

"We can talk about everything when we see you," I said. "Would it be possible to meet tonight or tomorrow night?"

"Yes, of course," Jake said. "Can you join us here? These days I rather prefer quiet times at home. You know I turned seventy-four this year, I find I don't enjoy as much the full business and social calendar that used to occupy my days and nights.

"In fact," he added, "why don't you and your lovely wife join us for dinner tomorrow night? I have such fond memories of when she and Linette seemed to be at our house day in and day out, back when they were students at St. Rose Academy. Time does fly, doesn't it? Shall we say tomorrow evening at 7:00?

"I will make sure that Louie knows you are joining us. I recall that your wife loved his famous Chinese cheese toasties when she was a school girl, but I'll have him prepare something more appropriate for tomorrow." He chuckled.

"That's perfect, Jake," I said. "Thank you and we'll see you tomorrow night."

Chapter 20   Wednesday, April 15, 1942

I worked in my study all morning, answering over a dozen letters — from the Knights of Columbus, asking for donations for the war bond drive; from the National Council of Catholic Men, requesting my attendance at the upcoming regional meeting, and asking me to offer the keynote address; from the St. Mary's College Alumni Association, asking me to preside over the award ceremonies at this year's commencement, and on and on.

I was glad to hear Flora call up to me that lunch was ready. After a delicious lunch of Flora's *Risotto con porcini*, complemented with a glass of Barbera, she served us *Panna cotta* topped with her canned apricots. We discussed tomorrow's dinner at the Osters over our espresso.

"How do you think we should do this?" I asked.

"Let's wait until after dinner, then ask Linette to tell her dad that she asked you for help," Flora said.

"Brilliant, we can then ask Louie Chen to provide us with the details of what happened."

"But of course, Commissioner," she joked. "We can hear what they have to say and save our own questions for when they seem most appropriate."

I had just returned to my study to finish my correspondence when the telephone rang. "Tony, this is Dennis, I'm calling from a phone booth in the Fairmont Hotel. I checked out Winthrop's boat early this morning and what I found there is troubling. And I just finished walking through his apartment. I think you and Ruthie need to go back there with me."

"Good work," I said. "Can you get back in the apartment without attracting attention during the day?"

"Yes, that won't be a problem. I've got to hang up now. There's a line of guys waiting to use this telephone — I've never seen the hotel so filled with people. Wait 'til you see his apartment. You won't believe it."

"I'm at home now," I said. "I could meet you there this afternoon if you think we can get in and out of the place unobtrusively during broad daylight. What about Ruthie? Do you want me to call and see if she is free?"

"That would be fine. I will get myself some lunch now and plan to meet you in front of 1298 Sacramento Street at 4:00. Ruthie should be at the art school working this afternoon, you can reach her there."

It's interesting that Dennis knows Ruthie's schedule so well, I thought, as I hung up the phone.

The receptionist at the California School of Fine Arts put me on hold for about a minute. "Hello? Who is this?" Ruthie finally answered.

"Hello, Ruthie. This is Tony. Can you meet me and Dennis at 4:00 in front of Winthrop's apartment house?"

"Sure, Tony. I'll get somebody to cover for me at the art school early and I'll see you there."

A chilly wind pushed the clouds eastward toward the Berkeley hills. It was one of those mid-April days in San Francisco that feels more like winter. I put on my charcoal gray fall and winter suit with a vest and took my light topcoat out of the closet.

Flora was surprised to see me dressed to go downtown, so I told her about Dennis's telephone call and our plan to meet with

Ruthie and look at Harlan Winthrop's place in the Chambord Apartments.

"Be careful, Tony," she said. "I'll see you when you come home."

I put on my hat, pecked her on the cheek and went outside to get my car.

I parked a few blocks down the North Slope of Nob Hill on the edge of North Beach. As I walked up Taylor Street to Sacramento I could see the reddish brown Pacific Union Club, housed in the only old time mansion still standing after the earthquake and fire in '06. My Catholic friends and I call it the "P.U." club. Catholics, especially Italian Catholics, are not welcome as members.

At one of the dinners put on to raise money for the 1939 Treasure Island fair, Harlan Winthrop surprised the rest of us sharing his table by holding up the new copy of the Social Register and proudly pointing to his entry. We gave each other that particular look reserved for when one of your peers drinks too much and behaves inappropriately.

As I turned West on Sacramento and walked to Winthrop's apartment, I realized he only had to go two short blocks to his club. I could never walk up here without remembering how the big earthquake and fire destroyed the mansions of Leland Stanford, Charles Crocker and most of the rest of them. I don't know the Bible by heart but I recalled those lines from Ecclesiastes: "A generation goes, a generation comes, but the earth remains forever."

The new generation in the form of Ruthie and Dennis were waiting for me at the Chambord Apartments. Ruthie was wearing her red outfit today, her beret pitched at a jaunty angle. Dennis wore the maroon tie and pocket handkerchief with his new gray chalk-striped suit. The younger generation certainly like their colors.

"Shall we go in?" Dennis asked. As the elevator ascended to the fifth floor, he took his lock pick wallet out of his pocket. We got out in a small foyer. Dennis went to the door for the apartment on the Sacramento Street side. We stood between him and the elevator as he inserted the tool into the lock. In a few seconds, he was opening the door.

I followed Ruthie, locked the door, and we took in our surroundings. Light flooded into the large living room from the south-facing windows. To our left was a bedroom. To our right, a small kitchen and a bathroom right off the entry hall. *A generous amount of space for one person*, I thought. The walls in the entry hall were filled with framed paintings and drawings. A quick look told me that they were mostly from the late Eighteenth and early Nineteenth centuries, and almost all were French.

"Wow," Ruthie said, "did you both see these pictures?"

"What do you mean?" Dennis asked.

"They're swell, but pretty racy, too! Look at this one," she said, pointing to a medium-sized engraving that occupied a central position on the wall across from the kitchen and bathroom. "Tony, I bet you don't have anything in your house that shows a fawn making love to a naked girl! None of my friends at the art school would submit this for the Art Commission show. And if it *were* accepted and shown, one of your Irish Catholic cops would surely arrest them."

Dennis chuckled. "As they say in the vaudeville shows, 'you ain't seen nothing yet.'"

Ruthie and I moved into the large oval-shaped living room. There were two bookcases, filled with dozens of antique-looking leather bound volumes and other more modern books. More paintings, a mix of oils, watercolors, and engravings, occupied most of the wall space. A huge oriental rug covered the floor. The furniture was either antique Louis XIV or excellent copies. A long table stood behind the sofa, which was covered in plum-colored heavy silk fabric. On the table was a glass case that contained a cavalry officer's sword with a small plaque that read: "This sword belonged to Friedrich von der Decken (1769-1840) during his service with The Kings German Legion, 1805-1807."

"I don't see what the big deal is," Ruthie said. "This was a rich old guy who liked old furniture and swords and racy old pictures, but is there anything else?"

"Come into the bedroom," Dennis said. We followed him into a medium size room furnished the same way, with a double bed, a dresser, and a desk. Above the desk was a small bookshelf. Dennis reached up and took two old, leather-bound books that looked very fragile. He handed one to me and one to Ruthie. On the front page, the title read *L'Histoire de Juliette, ou les Prospérités du vice* by The Marquis de Sade, 1797. The pages were yellowish brown in color and very brittle.

"I've heard of The Marquis de Sade, but I admit I never knew anything more than his name," Ruthie said. "This is really old! *Justine, ou Les Malheurs de la Vertu* — published in 1791. Tony, that's even before *your* time." She laughed. "Can you read French?"

"It looks like we have original copies of those infamous books, *The Misfortunes of Virtue* and *Vice Amply Rewarded*," I said.

"Let's trade," she said, taking my volume and giving me hers. "Do these old books have any pictures?" she asked, thumbing through the *Juliette* book.

"Oh, my," she cried, her clear pale complexion turning bright red. She closed the book and awkwardly put it down on the desk.

"Those pictures you just saw, Ruthie, caused a scandal when they were first printed," I explained. "They are still among the most explicit violent pornography ever published."

"What I think we have to take even more seriously," Dennis said, "is what I found in Winthrop's desk."

From the wide shallow drawer at the top he showed us a folder with playbills and a glossy 8x10 black and white photo. The photo showed a nude young Chinese woman holding a large white balloon. The balloon had a handwritten inscription. "To Harlan, a connoisseur of all things Oriental, Amber Lowe." The playbills were from The Forbidden City and The Chinese Sky Room, advertising scantily clad young female Chinese dancers.

There was also an article from a year ago cut from a magazine. The title read "How a Chinese Strip Tease Dancer Helps to Defeat Japan." Photos of two young women wearing next to nothing illustrated the story about the dancers sending their earnings back to China to aid the war effort.

Then Dennis opened the large drawer meant to contain letter size folders. He took out an ordinary modern book, a small ledger book bound in red leather, and several folders.

He put all these materials into a briefcase that stood next to the desk.

"I think we should take these with us and sit down somewhere where we can look at them in detail," he said. "There's something important here that we need to think about."

"That's okay by me," Ruthie said, her normal complexion slowly returning. "I'm getting sort of uncomfortable in here now. Let's get out of here."

Dennis opened the front door, looked to see that nobody was in the foyer, and we filed out. We took the elevator to the lobby and were back out on the sidewalk in a few minutes.

Chapter 21   Wednesday, April 15, 1942

Since it was still early enough, I suggested we make our way to the bar on the 19th floor of the Mark Hopkins Hotel and look through the materials that Dennis thought we needed to see. It was a cloudy day so not many people had come to enjoy the daytime view, and it was too early for the crowds who liked to see the downtown lights. We got a table right away. Ruthie asked for a Manhattan, Dennis and I ordered Scotch and soda. We nibbled on the nuts and pretzels that the waiter brought in a small, silver-plated dish.

"Dennis," I said, "I presume that you looked at these materials when you went to the apartment by yourself. What exactly do we have here?"

He reached into the briefcase and pulled out the book. It was an English translation of Adolph Hitler's *Mein Kampf.* He opened the front cover and showed us an inscription: "To Harlan Winthrop from his friend Charles Lindbergh, No War against the Master Race! Berkeley, California, April 19, 1940."

"That's really something," Ruthie said. "Lindbergh gave a speech at a big demonstration for peace over at the university — I'm sure it was that day. I was there, and so were my friends Esther and Barbara. We heard him speak. It was pretty thrilling, really, to see him in person like that."

Dennis frowned and shook his head. "If you look at the book, you can see that he read it and made lots of notes in the margins."

"That may well be," I said, "but it only shows that he was interested in Hitler's ideas. It doesn't say he was active against our country since Pearl Harbor. Besides, whoever *killed* him seemed to be on the side of the Axis, not *against somebody who favored the Axis,* if indeed Winthrop did."

"I agree, Tony," Dennis said. "This seems to be evidence that corroborates what you said were his public views about the strongest race being the White Anglo Saxons. But this other material, I'm not sure what to make of it."

The waiter came to the table and asked if we wanted a second drink. We all said yes.

Dennis pulled out the ledger book and opened it. The red leather cover was embossed with gold letters that read *Les Amis de Juliette.* He opened the ledger to a page with a list of names, addresses, and telephone numbers — all belonging to men. Then he turned to the back of the book. On the last several pages were lists of women's names, some of them Japanese and Chinese. There were "plus" signs and "minus" signs after some of the names.

The waiter put down our drinks and a new silver dish with nuts and pretzels. We each took a sip.

"I'm not sure what this means," Ruthie said. "The men must be members of the club, or whatever it is. But do we just assume the women are entertainers?"

"You could be a diplomat, Ruthie." I said, "Entertainers indeed!

"I've seen something like this," I continued. "When I was on the police commission we confiscated ledger books from some of the Madams who operated bordellos. They contained the names of their customers and listed the girls who worked in the bordello. My guess would be that Harlan and some of his friends were indicating their rating of some girls whose company they enjoyed."

"Huh," Ruthie said, "boy, you do have a way with words, Tony. After seeing those drawings, I wonder if that's how Harlan Winthrop would've described it."

"And here's something else," Dennis said, taking three folders out of the briefcase. He opened one of the folders to show a stack of glossy studio-quality 8x10 black and white photographs of nude, or nearly nude women, all Chinese. The first six photos had no identifying information. The bottom four had handwritten notes on the backs reading "Candid Camera, Treasure Island, 1939."

"Should we be looking at this stuff right here in the bar?" Ruthie asked. "Everybody was talking about the Sally Rand Dude Ranch and the Candid Camera at the Fair. But me and my friends refused to go to them — a bunch of dirty old men were always lined up to pay their money for a cheap thrill."

Dennis closed the folder and turned to the next one. "This one contains a deed to his boat *Juliette* — maybe that's the boat you saw him piloting, Tony. I went to the Marina this morning and went on board the boat. Somebody vandalized it — a window on the cabin door is broken, there's damage on the dashboard and there's stuff thrown around in the cabin."

"Do you think that's where Winthrop was killed?" I asked.

"We need to do a closer examination. It could have been a fight or it could just have been some vandals. That happens a lot down there. The harbormaster is a lazy old guy who does a bad job of security."

"Well, we have to get down there," I said.

Dennis held up another folder. "This one contains a property deed for a house in Sausalito."

"I think we need to visit this other house," I said. "So far we've found nothing in his apartment that helps us locate Winthrop's killer. I have to leave for another engagement now, but let's meet tomorrow."

Chapter 22   Thursday, April 16, 1942

I slept poorly, dreamt about things I cared not to remember, and woke up before dawn. Flora was still asleep so I went downstairs, made espresso, and picked up my newspapers. I was pleased to see there were no articles in Eddie Sarno's paper this week about me or the mayor. I made a mental note to telephone Mack and Barry and thank them for making my life a little more pleasant.

I drank my espresso and read *The Chronicle* as the sun slowly lit up the Marina district. The grim federal prison on Alcatraz Island looked better in the sunlight.

As soon as the clock showed 8:00 I called Dennis, and then Ruthie to ask them to meet me at the Harbormaster's office at the St. Francis Yacht Harbor as soon as possible. They each said they could be there by 9:00, so I quickly showered and shaved, took a clean shirt from my closet, and dressed in last night's outfit.

Flora was in the kitchen when I finished dressing. She asked me if I wanted breakfast, but I told her I would wait until later.

"I have to go meet Dennis and Ruthie. We have two tasks we need to do right away. The first is to look at Harlan Winthrop's boat, and the second is to drive to Sausalito to check out a second house we found out about."

"Remember we're having dinner with the Osters," Flora said.

I promised that I'd be back in time and kissed her goodbye.

Dennis and Ruthie were waiting at the Yacht Harbor. I had told them to dress comfortably given what we had to accomplish.

Dennis was wearing his leather jacket over a red and black plaid cotton shirt, khaki color hunting and fishing pants, and brown leather brogues like mine.

Ruthie gave me a start — she was dressed in trousers like the actress in *The Philadelphia Story*. Ruthie's long lustrous hair reminded me of her too. She wore a short light brown jacket over a dark blue blouse. Instead of her beret, she was wearing a baseball cap, dark blue like her blouse, with the San Francisco Seals team emblem depicting what Flora would probably describe as a cute little orange seal on the front.

We went to the Harbormaster's little house, knocked on the door, and walked into the office. A man in his sixties, navy blue boating blazer too small to accommodate his paunch, stood behind a counter. His florid face showed the usual lines and wrinkles you would expect after years spent out of doors. A blossom of gin flowers decorated his prominent nose. He was wearing a dirty white yachtsman's hat with an emblem of an anchor on the front and seemed surprised to see us. "How can I help you?" he asked, with a hint of suspicion. I noted his decidedly unfriendly gaze as he looked Ruthie up and down.

"I'm Police Commissioner Bosco," I said, not bothering to include the "former" — this person didn't require such detail, I decided. "This is Detective Sullivan and Detective Fuller," I added, offering Ruthie a sort of battlefield commission on the spot.

"We have instructions from Chief O'Reilly to search one of the boats berthed here — the *Juliette*."

"Hello Commissioner, the detective was here yesterday," he said, turning to Dennis. "He went aboard Harlan Winthrop's craft already, but if you need to go aboard again, be my guest."

He walked from behind the counter, took a large ring of keys from his belt, and said, "Follow me, I'll take you to the *Juliette*."

We walked along the sidewalk that ran parallel to Marina Boulevard from the Harbormaster's house toward the Presidio, passing several gates to gangways that angled down to a floating dock where the yachts were moored. He stopped in front of a gate marked "Number 6" and unlocked it. We followed him to the floating dock, then turned and walked past two cabin cruisers to one he pointed out. He took a key from his key ring, handed it to me, and said, "This will unlock the cabin doors. Bring it back to me when you finish. The gate above will automatically lock when you leave." Without another word he walked back the way we came.

"This is a pretty big boat," Ruthie said, "but it's smaller than some of them that we passed back there."

"According to the deed," Dennis said, "it's thirty-six feet in length, and has a cabin that sleeps two people, a small kitchen that they call a galley on a boat, and a small toilet, or head."

I stepped over the side onto the deck and immediately could see a large area of dark brownish staining. Dennis and Ruthie joined me as I unlocked the cabin.

The inside of the wheelhouse was a mess. Nautical charts were strewn about. On the floor lay a fire extinguisher alongside a telescope that extended all the way out and was bent out of shape. One of the glass panels on the side of the wheelhouse was shattered, its pieces scattered on the floor.

"Let me show you something I found below," Dennis said. He ducked his head and walked down the two steps that led to the cabin. "One of the cushions was pulled off the berth but there's something else of interest.

"Look what I found in the head." He walked back up into the wheelhouse holding a small towel. "Take a whiff of this," he said, handing it to me.

I smelled some kind of medicinal odor. "If this is what I think it is," I said, "this towel had Chloroform on it. The condition of the wheelhouse is such that some fighting obviously took place here."

"This is giving me the creeps!" Ruthie said, "Besides I don't like the way this boat is moving all the time. Can we get back on the land now?"

We locked the cabin and walked back to the Harbormaster's house. "I'm going to send two patrolmen down here to impound the boat, so keep that key handy for them," I said. "Did you see anyone going onto Winthrop's boat? It's obvious somebody was down there, somebody has trashed the boat, and it looks like there's dried blood on the deck."

"I haven't seen Mr. Winthrop. He doesn't usually come around until the season begins."

"Have you seen anyone else?" Dennis asked.

"Well, except for some workmen getting boats ready for the first day of the season next month, the only *owner* I've seen recently was Mr. Oster."

"Jake Oster?" I asked. "When did you see him?"

"Oh, I don't know for sure. A few weeks ago, I guess. He has a berth not too far from Mr. Winthrop's."

"Did you talk to him? Do you know why he was here?"

"I don't know why he was here. I just saw him from my office here and we waved to each other. It was early in the morning, just getting light."

"All right," I said. "Thanks for the help."

"Okay, and you can do what you want with Mr. Winthrop's boat, it's fine with me," he said. "I don't know why you are impounding it and frankly I don't care. But what about his car? It's been sitting there parked on the Boulevard for more than two weeks. People are starting to ask questions. It's a Packard Super Eight station wagon."

"I'll have the SFPD tow it away," I answered before we left his office.

From the telephone booth next to the Harbormaster's house I called in the orders to impound the boat and tow the car.

"I brought a police issue map of Sausalito," Dennis said as we all got into my car — Dennis in the front and Ruthie in the back. "The house is at the end of Theron Lane, below the highway at the top of the hill over there. Just drive across the bridge and then through the tunnel and take the first Sausalito road we come to."

As we drove onto the Golden Gate Bridge, we saw sentries on both sides of the highway. They were wearing long wool overcoats to ward off the chill of the winds blowing in from the Pacific. Rifles from the Great War rested on their shoulders. Most of the traffic on the bridge was headed into the city, so we made good time. Once we entered Sausalito, we wound our way to Theron Lane through an area that felt more like country than town. The house sat off all by itself at the very end of a lane occupied more by trees and bushes than other houses. It was a large two story brown shingle affair that looked as though it had been simply uprooted and transplanted to this site from the hills north of the campus of the university in Berkeley.

As though she had read my mind, Ruthie said, "This place looks just like Professor Szasz's Berkeley house. Look, it even has those big smooth gray rocks on both sides of the front stairs and a chimney made out of the same rocks!"

Evergreen trees and venerable oaks grew thickly on the property all around the house except for the gravel driveway that led to the front stairs and to a separate garage to the left. Dennis used his lock pick tool and we stepped into a vestibule that opened into a large living room and adjoining dining room. A mannequin of an English knight wearing a full suit of armor from the 1500s stood guard in the vestibule. Flora and I had seen one like it in London.

The floors were polished oak, decorated with Bokhara oriental carpets in several shades of red. Except for one small sofa in front of the fireplace, the rooms were unfurnished, as if to accommodate dancing. Bookshelves filled with erotic literature from Europe and Asia were built into the walls on both sides of the fireplace. The paintings and engravings in the living and dining rooms all depicted battles in which the Habsburg and Russian armies had defeated their revolutionary opponents in 1848 and 1849. One large oil painting foregrounded Russian soldiers dancing jigs and drinking mugs of beer as the thirteen "Martyrs of Arad" awaited their execution by hanging in the background. Another oil was a portrait of Otto von Bismarck age 43, with a virile mustache, wearing an Iron Cross insignia.

The house was cold. It lacked a lived-in feeling. The kitchen appeared to be rarely used.

A faint smell of incense surrounded us as we walked through the first floor rooms and went upstairs. In each of the four bedrooms, double beds occupied the center of the room. The walls were decorated with framed paintings and drawings of naked men and women participating in various intimate amorous activities. Each of the bedrooms contained a shelf with what appeared to be armamentaria for diverse types of erotic exploits, the depiction of which had caused Ruthie to blush and lose her emotional footing when she paged through Winthrop's copy of *Juliette*.

"I think we've seen enough, don't you?" I said, thinking to spare her similar discomfort.

Feeling subdued, we quietly returned to my Buick. No one spoke as we drove along the highway until we had passed through the tunnel heading down Waldo Grade to the Golden Gate Bridge. Ruthie broke the silence. "Look at that — San Francisco looks like a fantasy in a fairy tale."

I couldn't disagree. The dark greens of the Presidio in the foreground. Mount Sutro in the background. I thought of the World's Fair as I admired the sun shining on the old Fine Arts building. The downtown office buildings showed off their muted colors, and there was Coit Tower, standing out like a big white candle on top of a pastel birthday cake.

# Chapter 23	Thursday, April 16, 1942

I dropped off Dennis and Ruthie at the Marina and drove back to Pacific Heights, parked in front of our house, and went inside to change for dinner with the Osters. Flora had on a brown wool skirt with pleats and a beige cardigan sweater over a white blouse. She wore the pointed collars outside the sweater in the currently fashionable style. Instead of slip-ons, she had on a pair of dark brown lace-up walking shoes.

"Tony," she said, "you should change into something less businesslike, and you'd better hurry. We're supposed to be there before 7:00."

"I'll be quick," I answered as I walked up the stairs to the bedroom. I traded my suit, white shirt, and tie for gray gabardine slacks with what Flora called my "English gentleman's outfit" — a windowpane plaid shirt, brown tweed sports coat, and a pair of brown Church's brogues that we purchased on Jermyn Street during our last trip to London.

"Flora," I said, "I think we have enough time to simply walk to the Oster apartment, it's only a few blocks after all, and it's still light out."

The front yards in our neighborhood were a riot of color. I felt cheered up by the maple trees along the sidewalks wearing their intense yellow-green. Madame Alfred Carriere pinkish-white climbing roses. Deep purple clematis. White calla lilies and tulips of all colors.

"Tony," Flora said, "I feel so bad about the Japanese being sent away. I worry about Mr. Wada, our gardener."

"I know," I said. "Thousands of innocent people are being

hurt by the decision the president made to send the Japanese to camps out in the desert. What makes it even worse is that the FBI told him that it isn't necessary. Sometimes I think Jack Neylan has a point when he calls Roosevelt 'the enemy of mankind' because of his overuse of his presidential powers."

"I don't recall you ever agreeing with Neylan," Flora said.

I thought back to how I fought with Neylan during the big waterfront strike. I told him it was wrong to call the union men Reds. He should have known that most of them were good Catholics and the ones that weren't Catholics just wanted a decent wage, not a revolution.

"Oh, yes," I said, "Jack was livid when I refused to go along with him. He was still working for Hearst then." I recalled how Mayor Rossi objected to my criticizing Neylan and the ship owners for pressuring the newspapers to all print the same false story — that the dockworkers union was nothing but a Commie plot. I still find myself disagreeing with most of what Neylan says. But I agree with him that FDR is sometimes much too quick to issue his Executive Orders. Especially this one.

But I had warm feelings for Jake Oster. He believes, like I do, in a moral economy, with the business owners, the workers, and the government working as partners, for the good of all. His employees even made him an honorary member of their union years ago, because he was always on their side.

Of course, the Reds always hated that idea. According to them, it's all about ruling class against the working class. To hear them say it, Jake was against unions when in reality he was only against their Communist unions!

We entered the stylish Art Deco lobby and took the elevator to the Osters' penthouse apartment. Jake answered the door and greeted us warmly. I was struck by how youthful he looked, though his hair was now thin and white, not thick and blond. Like many men in their seventies, he'd shrunk a little and lost some weight, but his face was relatively free of lines. His body was muscular and firm-looking with a good color and he had a strong handshake.

"Flora," he said, "my, how good it is to see you. And you look absolutely gorgeous! If I didn't know different, I'd think you were a student dropping by to interview an old man about his career in San Francisco business."

Flora blushed. "Hello, *Jake* — see, I didn't call you Mr. Oster," she said.

We followed Jake into the living room, with its sweeping 9th floor panoramic view of the Marina district, the Bay, Angel Island, the Marin hills, and the Golden Gate Bridge. Mildred came out of the dining room with Linette and they both said hello.

"Please sit down," Mildred said. "Since it's spring, Louie is making us a roast lamb dinner. And in honor of you two from Northern Italy, he's experimenting with an Italian dessert — tiramisu. I told him how much I enjoyed your recipe, Flora, and he said he wanted to see if he could make one to your liking."

I told Mildred that I'd never seen the collection of handheld fans that she was displaying in a case along one wall of the living room. "I have been collecting these since the first time we went to Japan, over twenty-five years ago," she said. "Now I have samples from Europe *and* the Orient, and Jake surprised me by having this glass case made for some of my fans."

"I asked one of the people at the DeYoung Museum to make it for us," Jake added. "We've arranged to have our entire collection of Asian and European fans donated to the museum when we pass."

"Except for those pieces that your daughter wants to keep, right, Father?" Linette said with a smile.

Jake chuckled. "Well, yes, of course. Tony, you and Flora don't need to think of such things quite yet."

Just then, a bell tinkled from the dining room. Louie Chen, wearing an apron over his white shirt and black bow tie, his round face beaming, was ringing a symphony-quality triangle and calling us to the table.

"It's very good to see you, Miss Flora," Louie said.

"Oh, Louie," Flora said, "I'm so happy to see you, too. I can't wait to taste your tiramisu!"

Louie's cooking had only gotten better over the years. I enjoyed the roast lamb garnished with rosemary that he grew himself and his homemade mint jelly. "Louie, if you keep this up we'll have to start calling you 'Luigi'," I said, complimenting his tiramisu.

He laughed, bowed, and said, "*Grazie mille, Dottore!*"

As Violet, the Oster's maid, cleared away the dishes, Louie went off to prepare some coffee. Jake turned to me. "I know we have something to discuss," he said, "so let's do it over coffee, shall we? Would you like to smoke? I can have Violet bring you an ashtray. We decided to stop smoking so we don't have ash-trays out like we used to."

"I'm considering quitting, too, and since you're not smoking and Flora never smokes, I'll pass tonight."

Linette, who had been somewhat subdued during the dinner conversation said, "Father, I think Louie should participate in this discussion, so can you have Violet make a place for him after he brings the coffee?"

"Why on Earth would we include Louie?" Jake said with a strained tone of voice. "I thought you wanted to discuss the race relations resolution you and Flora presented at your meeting."

Linette's brow furrowed and she reddened. "No, Father, it's not about our resolution at all. And you are going to be angry, because you told us that Louie's problem had to be kept secret. I'm sorry, but I just couldn't keep this all to myself. I told Flora, and then I told Tony, too."

Jake's face was red. His blue eyes took on a piercing look. His fists were clenched on the table on either side of his coffee cup and saucer. In a low, measured voice he said, "Linette, I'm surprised you shared what is private family business with Flora and Tony. It would not be fair to them to involve them in this matter."

Flora, Mildred and I sat silently. I had almost stopped breathing. Linette stood up abruptly and shouted, "Father, I'm a grown woman with children, not a child. I will not be silent about this! I shared this with Flora and Tony because Flora is my oldest friend and Tony is a lawyer and former police commissioner. He was a member of the Board of Supervisors. He will know what to do about all of this better than any of us. I wish you had asked his advice when all of this started." Her voice softened. "I know you mean well, but my conscience will not let me be silent about this."

Violet was standing by the door with a tray holding the coffee urn. "Violet, please just put the urn on the table and bring a chair for Louie," Mildred said. "Please ask Louie to come into the dining room and join us." She turned to her husband. "Jake," she said, "Linette is right. We cannot just sweep this all under the rug."

"Please let Tony tell us what he thinks we should do," Linette said. "I'm not being hysterical, so please don't say that I am. I will go along with whatever Tony thinks is right, but I think we need to have his opinion."

Mildred said, "Jake, think about it like asking a doctor for a second opinion just to make sure the first diagnosis was the right one. It just seems like the most sensible thing to do and I know you are a sensible man."

Jake was slowly shaking his head, looking down at the table, his face still reddened. Several minutes passed before he finally spoke. "I am very sorry this has happened, Tony and Flora. I'm not pleased with you, Linette. We are certainly not going to discuss this matter here and now." He turned to me, "I'll call you in the morning, Tony. You and I can have a talk.

"Linette, please sit down. Violet, please serve the coffee. Let's not spoil this pleasant evening."

Chapter 24   Friday, April 17, 1942

Flora and I were finishing our breakfast when the doorbell rang.

"Who could that be so early?" Flora asked. "It's not even 8:00 yet."

I walked to the front door and looked out. I was surprised to see Linette Bassano and Louie Chen in a sport coat and a fedora. I opened the door and invited them in.

"Good morning, Tony," Linette said.

Before I could reply, Louie took off his hat and said, "Good morning, Commissioner. We have come to talk to you about what happened last night. Can we come in?"

"Of course, pardon my manners, but I wasn't expecting you two. Please come in."

Flora had walked into the entry hall to join us. "What a surprise!" she said, her expression underscoring the point. "What's going on, Linette?"

"I'll let Louie tell you." Linette turned to Louie.

"Miss Flora and Commissioner," he said, "we came over because something odd happened this morning. We need to tell you about it."

"It's got to be related to that business I wanted to talk about last night," Linette said.

"Would you like coffee?" Flora asked. "We were just finishing our breakfast."

After they both declined, we went into the living room and sat down. "What happened this morning?" I asked.

Louie was holding his hat and now he put it on the coffee table in front of the sofa. "I was in the kitchen, about 5:00 as usual every morning. I was mixing up the muffins that Mr. and Mrs. Oster have for breakfast every Friday."

"Those are delicious," Flora exclaimed. "I remember them."

Linette smiled, "Mother and Father still enjoy them. It's a tradition."

"Anyway," Louie continued, "Mr. Oster came into the kitchen. I was very surprised, because he never comes to the kitchen, and it was so early. He looked like he was tired and he seemed upset. He was all dressed and wearing his duck hunting jacket, the one with the big pockets in the front."

"That's odd," I said. "It's not anywhere near duck hunting season."

"I said that to him," Louie said. "He said, 'I know that, but I have to go out of town for a while and this jacket is comfortable.' Then he asked me to pack him sandwiches and to fill up his big Thermos jug with coffee."

"Where was he going?" I asked.

Linette shook her head, with a troubled look. "We don't know," she said. "Louie didn't ask Father where he was going. That would have been inappropriate."

"So I stopped making the muffins and made him his favorite sandwiches," Louie continued, "with roast beef and Limburger cheese. He went away and came back with his duffel bag and told me to come with him."

"Where did you go?" Flora asked.

"We took the elevator to the garage," Louie said. "When we got down there, we went to his station wagon and put everything inside."

"He doesn't usually drive anywhere by himself anymore," Linette said. "It's just so odd."

"He must have told your mother what's going on," Flora said to Linette.

"And that's the other thing that's so strange. Mother called me and said she woke up and Father was gone, and when she asked Louie if he'd seen Father, Louie told her what had happened."

"Jake was clearly upset last night," I said. "I think you're right that his behavior this morning must be related to what you wanted him to tell us, Linette."

"I think you're right, *Dottore*," Louie said. "I feel like Mr. Oster is upset because of me — well, me and my family."

"What do you mean, Louie?" Flora asked.

"Well, it's a long story, so let me explain. Maybe you know I converted to be Catholic after I worked for Mr. and Mrs. Oster for a couple years," Louie started. "I married my wife Elizabeth in St. Vincent de Paul Church. It was just down the street when the Osters had their house on Green Street, before they moved to their apartment. Elizabeth and I lived upstairs in the Oster house in those days. Then we had our girl Mary and we moved to Chinatown. Then we had our boy Christian. Mary and Christian went to the parish school, then Mary attended George Washington High School. She graduated two years ago. Christian, he's a senior now at George Washington.

"We had many troubles with Mary. She was a strong-minded girl. She was always a good student, but she didn't want to go to church when she was in high school. She liked to be with the artists and the singers and dancers. So, Elizabeth and I said when you graduate from high school, you should go to college, be a teacher. Mary said, no she wanted to be a dancer and a singer.

"Finally, Elizabeth and I, we gave up. Then Mary went to the Fair on Treasure Island and to all the Gayway places and said, 'I want to be a dancer like, you know, that Noel Toy woman.'

"What could we do? She's eighteen and we couldn't stop her. She got a job to dance at Forbidden City and some other places in Chinatown. We said, okay, but you have to wait after shows for your brother and he will bring you back home. She didn't like this but she said okay, fine.

"One night after a show, a man Mary knew from the club was waiting for her. She knew his name from signing her pictures for him. Harlan Winthrop."

"Oh, my God," I heard myself exclaim, spontaneously. Louie looked at me, surprised at my outburst.

"Go ahead, Louie," I said.

"Well this man asked Mary to go for a ride," Louie said, "but she said no. Then he tried to put her in a car, to take her away. Christian tried to stop him, but the man had a gun and took him too. He took them to a boat.

"Mary and Christian tried to get away from the boat. Christian had to fight the man. He's a strong big boy. He was a football player and a wrestler. But Christian got tired, and the man had him on the deck of boat, choking him. Then Mary saw a knife and stabbed the man in his back to save her brother."

I knew that Louie was talking about the *Juliette.* "So what happened then?" I asked.

"Christian called me on the telephone, all upset. 'Father, what should we do?'"

"What *did* you do?" Flora asked.

"I asked Mr. Oster for help, and he drove me down to the Marina in his station wagon. We brought Christian and Mary home."

"What about the man who was stabbed?" Flora asked.

"Mr. Oster just left the body on the boat. He told us, 'Everything will be fine, we will keep this a secret, and nobody ever has to know.' We never saw anything about it in the paper, so we thought Mr. Oster was right."

Linette had been sitting quietly. Now she spoke up. "We don't know anything about the dead man. Louie was very worried about that. He was so upset that he told me this story when I was at the apartment the other day." She looked at me and Flora. "I just felt I had to tell you about it, because it just seemed wrong. I think my father ought to have called the police. I thought you'd know what to do."

I realized I had been taking shallow breaths as Louie told his story. "This is extraordinary," I said. "As Flora knows, I've been delegated by the Chief of Police to find this person's killer. Also, I'm sworn to secrecy, and the same is true of the detectives working with me.

"You're saying they killed the man in self-defense, but we need to make sure of that."

"Don't you believe me, *Dottore*?" Louie asked.

I turned to him. "Louie, I have no reason to doubt you or Christian and Mary, but I have to talk to them. The police should have been called right away. I'm surprised Jake didn't do that, frankly."

"You need to talk to Jake, then," Flora said. "Wasn't he supposed to call you this morning?"

"Yes, but now for whatever reason, he's left without telling anybody where he's going.

"What you've told me must be kept quiet," I said. "Louie and Linette, you did the right thing by sharing this with me and Flora. But I am going to insist that just as Jake wanted this to remain secret, so do I."

Louie nodded, and Linette said, "You know best, Tony. I feel much better now that we were able to talk to you about it."

"The chief delegated me to solve this murder case," I said, "but now it appears *it was not murder but self-defense*. Where are Mary and Christian? I will need to interview them and hear their side of the story."

"They are both at Mills College, in Oakland," Louie said. "Mr. Oster took them over there. The president of the college is a good friend of his."

"All right," I said. "Please remember that nothing has changed in the sense that this has to remain, as they say in the military 'Top Secret.'"

Louie and Linette stood up, and Louie put on his hat.

"I'll have to find Jake and hear his side of this story, too," I said. "I have an idea where he is. But first, I'll need to go to Mills College."

After they left, Flora said, "Do you really think you can find Jake? And why would he just leave town like this?"

"I could be wrong, Flora, but I'm betting that whatever is going on with Jake goes all the way back to days of the *First* World War."

Chapter 25   Friday, April 17, 1942

The Bay Bridge looked immune to natural or man-made damage, the spring sunshine making its silver-gray surfaces shine. But I knew that if we didn't protect it from Axis bombs, they could reduce it to an eight-mile-long pile of debris. I wondered how many of the thousands who crossed it every day gave a thought to just how vulnerable we might be to fifth column sabotage of our bridges.

"Do we need to stop for lunch before we drive to Mills College?" I asked.

"I'd rather go straight there," Dennis said.

"I'm not hungry," said Ruthie. "After what you just told us about this new development, I couldn't eat if you paid me."

I smiled. "Well that's settled. Besides it's a long drive."

"I figure if you add the eight miles of the bridge, Mills College should be about fifteen miles from downtown," Dennis said. "There's no highway to the college, so we have to drive through Oakland along MacArthur Boulevard most of the way."

Dennis and Ruthie had met me at our house, and we'd driven through the Marina and then through the industrial and warehouse district downtown to get to the bridge. As I drove up Rincon Hill onto the bridge, Ruthie said, "I've never gone across this in a car, only on the Key System train on the tracks underneath where the cars go. It always seemed dark going back and forth on the bridge. This is much better. What a fantastic view!"

"Wait until you see the city when you come out of the tunnel on the way back," Dennis said. "Talk about a fantasy in a fairy tale."

I had not driven to Oakland since Pearl Harbor. I imagined there would be more activity but I was not prepared for what we heard, saw, and smelled as we drove off the bridge into the harbor district. The air was filled with the harsh metallic clamor of the freight and passenger trains, belching smoke as they lined up to enter the West Oakland train yards. Long-distance trucks roared by, putting out stinking diesel fumes and more smoke as they drove into and out of the Oakland Army Base. We found ourselves stuck in the traffic and forced to experience the unsettling noise and the noxious environment for over thirty minutes.

"This place is changing just like the Fillmore," Ruthie said, as we finally got moving and drove past the train yards and then along Seventh Street toward the downtown. "This is much noisier and dirtier than where I grew up in the South of Market area."

"This part of Oakland is becoming like back East," Dennis said. "I took the train across the country and went to Pittsburgh. Everywhere, there were crowds, terrible smelly smoke. We don't realize what a great place San Francisco is because we were born here and we think — well, this is what life is like, but it's not at all!"

"I wasn't born in San Francisco," I said, "I came here when I was eleven years old. I agree it's a great place, but my little town in the Piedmont in Italy — well, that's paradise to me. That's why I go back whenever I can."

"Ha," Dennis said, "I remember Professor Hennessy at St. Mary's once told us something that Senator Phelan said in a speech. 'If I owned both heaven and California, I would live in California and rent out heaven.'"

"There's Lake Merritt on our right." We remained silent as we drove to the sylvan campus of Mills College nestled beneath the wooded hills of Crestmont and Redwood Heights.

A security officer in a guardhouse at the entrance gave us a visitor's pass. We followed his directions, driving about a quarter of a mile along a road lined with eucalyptus trees. I parked in front of a large four-story building that reminded me of St. Patrick's Seminary in Menlo Park but for the fact that it was made of wood and not bricks. I locked the car and we walked to the front door. When we stepped into the lobby, the resemblance to St. Patrick's got stronger — the antique grandfather's clock; the large portraits of past presidents of the institution; the two sofas and wing chairs for visitors.

I asked Dennis and Ruthie to make themselves comfortable. At an office with a sign reading "President," a secretary listened as I introduced myself and told her the reason for my visit. "Oh, yes," she said, "President Reinhardt is expecting you, and I believe your colleagues as well? Please take a seat in the lobby and the president will be with you in a few minutes."

We watched a dozen or so students walk by us on the way to their classrooms, the library, or the lunchroom. Just as I thought to myself that, judging by appearances, Ruthie would fit in here quite well, she said, "I feel old."

Before either Dennis or I could reply, a tall handsome woman in her sixties wearing an elegant gray-blue wool business suit with a long skirt, her brown hair drawn back in a loose bun, walked toward us, put out her hand to me and said, "You must be Commissioner Bosco. I'm Aurelia Reinhardt."

We shook hands and I introduced Dennis and Ruthie. She welcomed us to Mills College. "Come with me and we'll take a little walk." We followed her out the front door and along a pathway. "I'd like to show you something of our modest campus. You will see no men here," she said turning to Dennis with a smile. "We like to say, 'Mills College is not a school for girls without men; it's a school for women without boys.'"

"Ha, ha," Ruthie laughed, "I like you, President Reinhardt! I never heard anything like that at Berkeley. Just the opposite — I had the feeling the place was full of boys. They acted like the women were either invisible or put there so they could have fun at their expense."

"Well, perhaps you ought to have joined our community instead of the university. There's a great deal to be said for a women's college. We educate the future leaders of our country here."

"Tony and I went to a men's college," Dennis said, chuckling. "They told us over at St. Mary's that *we* were going to be the future leaders. So which of you are telling the truth, President Reinhardt?"

We all laughed and the president stopped in front of a bell tower, explaining that it was designed by one of the country's leading architects, a woman named Julia Morgan. "She designed Mr. Hearst's castle and some of the buildings in Berkeley, too — for example the Women's City Club. This is the bell tower she designed for us. Her work here provides our students with the inspiration to imagine themselves becoming future architects, scientists, mathematicians, and even, but certainly not only, teachers and good wives and mothers.

"There is so much I could show you," she added. "You can perhaps tell that I'm very proud of our institution and our women. But how can I help you?"

"From what we hear," I replied, "you have already been of great assistance to the two children of Louie Chen. You can assist us by allowing us to speak with Mary and Christian. We have a few questions to ask them about the events that led Jake Oster to bring them to you."

President Reinhardt turned around and headed back in the direction of her office. "One of my missions in life," she said, sounding very much like a professor or a priest, "is to aid the unfortunate. I was more than happy to help these two young people.

"As to how we might proceed," she said, "I am scheduled to attend a meeting that will take several hours and will include a luncheon, so I suggest that you simply use my office to interview, if that's the right word, Mary and Christian. I will send my secretary to locate them and bring them to my office. If you'd like, since it's lunch time, I can have our people bring over sandwiches and something to drink for all of you. Please make yourselves comfortable."

Chapter 26   Friday, April 17, 1942

"What a swell office," Ruthie said. "This sure is a far cry from the chief's dark little office in the Hall of Justice."

Sunlight flooded into the spacious room through floor to ceiling south-facing windows. The high ceiling made the space feel even larger. A sofa and several chairs were positioned around a coffee table at one end of the room, and at the other end were a mahogany desk and two visitor's chairs. Portraits of elegant women in academic gowns or ballroom attire from the past century hung on the walls.

Appearing energized by our surroundings, Ruthie walked to the desk. "The president told us to make ourselves comfortable," she said, "and I'm going to do like she says." She walked behind the desk, pulled out the wheeled leather arm chair, sat down and twirled it in a circle.

Just then, someone knocked on the door. "Come in," I said.

Two young students came in, one carrying a tray of sandwiches, apples, and oranges, the other a small cardboard box with bottles of Coca-Cola. "Set those on the table," I said, motioning to the coffee table.

"There are glasses in the cupboard there," said the student who put down the Coca-Cola, pointing to a Federalist style high cabinet with glass doors that matched the desk, the sofa, and the chairs.

"Well, I sure am hungry now." Ruthie took one of the sandwiches. Dennis and I joined her, sitting on the sofa at the other end of the room.

We were still eating our sandwiches and drinking the Co-ca-Cola when we heard another knock on the door. "I'll get it," Ruthie said, jumping up from her chair. "You must be Mary and Christian, come in!"

They slowly walked across the threshold appearing uncertain as to who they should be speaking to.

I walked over to them, introduced myself, Ruthie, and Dennis, and we all shook hands. Mary wore a pleated dark green plaid skirt, a navy blue cardigan sweater over a white blouse, bobby socks and brown and white saddle shoes. In contrast to Ruthie, she looked thin, and at about five-feet tall, she appeared tiny. Her college girl outfit did nothing to disguise the striking beauty of her unblemished delicate features. Christian reminded me of Louie. I could easily imagine him on the football and wrestling teams given his height at about five and a half feet and his impressively muscled upper body with a large chest and neck. He had an ugly bruise on the left side of his face, from above his eye to his chin.

"Please be seated on the sofa there," I suggested, "and we'll take the chairs." I looked meaningfully at Ruthie. She took the point, and — with a neutral expression — moved one of the desk side chairs over to the conversation area by the sofa.

I explained to Mary and Christian that their dad had given me a brief description of what had transpired on Palm Sunday.

"We both talked with our father this morning, Mr. Bosco," Mary said. "We were expecting you. But why do you need to talk to us? We would like to forget about what happened, not have to think about it all over again."

"Mary, you need to be patient," Christian said. "I feel like Mr. Bosco is on our side, or the police would already have arrested us for questioning."

"That's correct, young man," I said. "And your wanting to forget it all is understandable, but what you did, even if it *was* in self-defense, was a very serious matter."

Mary began to reply, but I cut her off and continued.

"We are sorry to put you through the pain and discomfort of having to describe your awful experience to us, but Chief O'Reilly has delegated us to investigate Harlan Winthrop's death. We need to know the details of what happened so we can decide how to proceed."

"He deserved what he got," Christian said with vehemence. "We don't believe in hurting animals, let alone people, but I don't feel guilty about what happened to him!"

"I feel the same way," Mary said. "Are you going to arrest us? My father told us that no one would ever have to know about what happened."

"You and Christian are probably not going to be arrested, Mary. *Provided you did kill Harlan Winthrop in self-defense.* Your dad explained the arrangements he made for you here at Mills College, and that should all be just fine. But we need you to tell us in your own words what happened. Can you both be patient and do that for us?

"Perhaps you could start at the beginning and tell us about your dancing, Mary," I suggested. "Your dad told me that you've always liked to dance."

"Yes," she said, "and when I was a junior at George Washington High School my dance teacher introduced me to some of the dancers at Charlie Lowe's club, The Forbidden City. Some of them were dancing at the Treasure Island fair. They told me I should join them at Forbidden City. I could make lots of money, but my parents wouldn't let me do it."

"They had some big noisy arguments," Christian said. "They said those dances are sinful and it would bring great shame to our family if Mary did anything like that."

"So I just had to wait until I was eighteen," Mary said, "and I danced all over after that. Forbidden City, Chinese Sky Room, Dragon's Lair, Lion's Den, Club Shanghai, even the Kubla Khan. I never used my real name — my dad would have had a heart attack. Anyway, they like us to have fancy names. I was many things, but I liked Lily of the Valley the best, and since last Thanksgiving I've been dancing at the Cellar Club."

"But my dad made me be her bodyguard, or something like that," Christian said. "He's old now, but if he makes up his mind about something, you better look out. I couldn't tell him no and neither could Mary."

"He showed me something he cut out of one of the papers about Forbidden City," Mary said. "Remember, Christian?"

"It was something like 'Charlie Lowe's girls are stolen by lovesick swains' — we had to look up the word, remember, Mary? It was an article about dancing girls falling in love with customers and moving to other cities. But my dad, he thought it was about girls being kidnapped. He said I had to go with her and then when she finished after the show I had to meet her and bring her home. It was no big deal, we live in Chinatown, but it was a nuisance."

"But after that he sort of forgot about it," Mary said. "I always gave him ten percent of whatever I earned — for our poor relatives, right? He liked that because it's Chinese Confucian tradition. He always told us we have to be good Chinese in the traditional Confucian way and good Christians, too. Okay, okay, I'm an American, right, but I just go along with this stuff even if it's really boring."

"Well," I said, "I'm getting a feel for the whole dancing business, and I'm wondering what happened on the night of Palm Sunday?"

"Everything was fine until I came out on the sidewalk after the show," Mary said. "One of the men who come to the Cellar Club was standing on the sidewalk — a handsome sort of older guy who came to a lot of my shows. I just thought he was waiting for somebody. Christian was still inside the club."

"I was pretty much right behind you but stopped to say goodbye to Minnie," Christian said.

"She's one of the other dancers," Mary explained. "Anyway I was standing there waiting for Christian and this man, he said, 'May I take you for a little spin in my Packard?' He comes to the club all the time. I thought, this guy is weird, what a stupid line, and just said no and smiled and kept waiting for Christian."

"And I'm just starting to come out the door," Christian said, "and I see this guy pull something out of his topcoat and come over to Mary, and he grabs her around the waist with his left arm and takes his right hand with what now I see is a small towel. He puts it over her face and starts dragging her to a car parked there."

"I'm smelling this horrible stuff, and kicking and struggling with this guy," Mary said, "but he's big and strong and kind of pulling me backwards. It made me feel sick, horrible."

"I yelled at the guy 'Hey, what are you doing, that's my sister!'" Christian said. "And he just dropped Mary on the sidewalk, dropped the towel, and took a gun out of his suit pocket.

He pointed it at me and said, 'Shut up, kid, and get over here.' So what could I do? I didn't want him to shoot me, so I went over to where Mary was on the sidewalk moaning.

"Nobody was out there, it was just him and us. He said, 'Open the Packard there, get in the driver's seat and close the door' — I don't know how he knew I could drive, but most kids my age do, so he must have just guessed that I did. I was really scared I guess. I just did what he said. He was holding the gun on me all the time."

Mary said, "He opened the back of his station wagon and made me get in there. I had to lie down. Then he put the towel on me again, for a long time it seemed like. I kind of blacked out then."

"He told me to drive," Christian said. "He held the gun on me and made me drive out to the Marina and park. He made me get Mary out of the way back of the station wagon. She was kind of groggy but she could sort of walk if I helped her. He put the towel in his pocket and had the gun out again. He told us to walk to this gate, then he unlocked it and made us walk down to the boats.

"He made us get into this one boat, and then he got on it. He unlocked the door and started to go inside, and we were still outside on the deck. He had to bend over to get inside the boat and he had the gun in his left hand, so I kicked him as hard as I could. He flew forward, one of his feet caught on the piece of wood that separates the inside from the deck —"

"That's the threshold," I said.

"Okay, right, so he tripped on that thing and flew forward when I kicked him from behind. I'm a strong kicker, okay? I'm good at field goals. Anyway, he dropped the gun and hit his head on the steering wheel in there. As he was starting to get up, I moved closer to him and tried to punch him, but he blocked me even though he wasn't standing all the way up yet."

"I could hear them from the deck," Mary said, "and I was trying to wake up but I was all woozy."

"He was really strong for an older guy," Christian said, "and we were hitting at each other for a long time, you know inside that cabin. He picked up a telescope that was on a shelf in front of the steering wheel and slugged me with it — you can see he hit me really hard, I still have this big bruise. I pulled a fire extinguisher off the wall near the steering wheel and hit him, but he blocked that, too. I tried to use a wrestling hold on him that I learned at school — I'm a good wrestler — but I couldn't put him down and we were in this sort of clinch and hit the doorway and we staggered through the door out onto the deck outside still trying to throw each other.

"Then he did a real dirty trick. He kneed me, you know where, as we were clinched up like that and he got me down on my back and started choking me."

Mary said, "That's when I saw a place on the side of the boat out there where three knives were in a sort of rack. I was not so groggy anymore. I didn't even think, I pulled out the biggest knife and I just stabbed him as hard as I could in his back."

"He let go of my neck all of a sudden," Christian said, "so I pushed up with all my strength, and got out from under him. I pushed him back on his stomach and he was moaning, but then he was quiet. Blood was coming out of him and the deck was getting all bloody."

"So how did you get word to your dad?" I asked.

"We didn't know what to do," Mary said. "There was nobody around. So at least nobody saw us or saw what happened. Christian told me we should call our dad, so he gave me a nickel and stayed there and I walked to a little house made of stones. There was a telephone booth there, so I called my dad. He said to just wait by the phone, and after a while, it seemed like forever, our dad and Mr. Oster came."

"Mr. Oster drove us right over here," Christian said.

"What about the man on the boat?" I asked. "What did you do with the body?"

"We don't know anything about that," Mary said, shaking her head. "Mr. Oster didn't talk about it. Just thinking about it makes me upset again."

"I think Mr. Oster did something with the body of that guy," Christian said. "I probably should have asked him, or asked my dad. But, you know, our family is used to letting Mr. Oster take care of whatever needs doing. He's always been really generous to us over the years."

"You must have been in shock, too," Ruthie said.

"Anyway, President Reinhardt was waiting for us here. She gave us rooms in one of these old buildings here. The next day she told us the whole plan."

"I couldn't believe it!" Mary said. "I will be able to get my college degree here *in dancing*! Mr. Oster is paying for everything."

"And I can finish up my high school diploma by mail," Christian said. "Mr. Oster has fixed it all up. My dad said he would sign off on my enlisting in the Navy now, but I want to have my diploma and then enlist. So that's what I'll do and in the meantime I get to learn cooking from the chef here at Mills College."

Dennis, Ruthie, and I looked at each other. "Thank you, Mary and Christian," I said. "We will make sure all of this is communicated directly to the chief."

"We may be able to arrange that no charges will be filed against you," Dennis said, "but until we contact you about that, I have to insist that you don't leave town."

"We understand," Christian said.

"In the meantime," I looked at Mary, "try to forget what happened as much as humanly possible and get on with your lives. I speak for all three of us when I congratulate you both on your bravery and your ability to cope with such a terrible experience.

"Ruthie, would you like to say something to Mary and Christian before we leave?" I asked.

She smiled. "Well, you guys, as a famous man once said to me, 'We have to go on, or we'll go under.' Right, Commissioner?" She tilted her head slightly and made a crooked smile. "And you guys" — she turned to Mary and Christian — "are doing a great job, so keep it up, and remember," she made a V sign, "Victory!"

Chapter 27   Friday, April 17, 1942

We said goodbye to Mary and Christian and walked from the president's office to the lobby. I suggested we sit down in the comfortable chairs and gather our thoughts. The antique grandfather clock ticked off the minutes.

Dennis was shaking his head. "We seem to have spent a lot of time and energy looking for Harlan Winthrop's killer in all the wrong places. The chief won't be happy."

"Yes," I said, "but if what Mary and Christian have told us is all true, we're close to solving this case."

Ruthie sighed. "So we have to find out for sure how the body got into Coit Tower. And that RoBerTo sign on the wall. Where do we go from here, boss?"

"Actually," I laughed, "though you probably didn't mean it this way, we have to go to Suisun Bay."

"What are you talking about, Tony?" Dennis said.

"Where is *that?* Ruthie asked.

"Contra Costa County. I think Jake is up there and we need to talk to him before we meet with O'Reilly."

"So we're now thinking that Jake was involved in putting Winthrop's body in Coit Tower?" Dennis asked.

"Yes, and I think I know why, but until we can interview him it's just a hunch."

"Well, we need to get going then. My badge doesn't give me any official authority there, but at least I'm not just a private citizen like you and Ruthie," Dennis said.

"You guys are not leaving me out," Ruthie announced.

"Here's what I know," I said. "According to his daughter and Mary and Christian's dad, Jake left his house early this morning. He didn't call me like he said he would, and he didn't tell anyone where he was going. I think he may have had a nervous breakdown."

"That would explain why he didn't clean up the boat after he put Winthrop's body in Coit Tower," Dennis said.

"Yes. He's in his mid-seventies, after all. He looks fit and healthy, but he's been through some shocking events. I'm betting he's gone up to his duck hunting club. It's a private club. I've been there several times with him and one of my predecessors on the police commission, Andrew Mahoney."

"My dad knew Mahoney," Dennis said. "He used to bring me chocolate bars when he came for dinner."

"Mahoney used to own Joice Island. It's not far from Jake's club and lots of other hunting clubs up there in the San Joaquin River Delta."

Dennis nodded. "My dad and some of my uncles belong to those clubs. They're old fashioned — no indoor plumbing, natural gas, or electricity."

"Why do you think Oster went there?" Ruthie asked.

"It seems logical because he was dressed in his hunting gear, and he had Louie make him sandwiches. That's what you would take if you were driving somewhere. He might think it would be a good place to get away from everything if this business gets into the papers. It's a hard place to get to, members keep it very private."

"What if you're wrong?" Dennis asked. "Maybe we should telephone up there and see if he made a reservation. That would save us a trip for nothing if he's not there."

"We don't want to take a chance that he'd leave if he knew we were coming. His club is like most of those in Suisun Bay and Grizzly Bay. It has a caretaker who lives at the club who picks you up and takes you to the island by boat. You can only get there by boat. If we called the caretaker ahead of time, we couldn't ensure he wouldn't tell Jake about it."

"I don't like boats." Ruthie grimaced. "That *Juliette* was awful, but I don't want to be left out."

"The boat trip is not that long, Ruthie, but I don't want you to go if you'll be uncomfortable."

"I'm not staying behind, boss! But if we can't call the caretaker how will we get to the island?"

"I'll call my cousin Alessandro. He lives in Martinez. He can meet us there and take us to the Marshall Island Duck Club on his fishing boat."

Dennis and Ruthie went to the student cafeteria to buy more sandwiches and Cokes.

I went to the telephone booth and called Alessandro, explaining that we needed a boat to take us to the duck club.

"Tony, they took away my boat. I can't take you anywhere," he said.

"You mean the Army?" I asked.

"Sure, the Army," he said angrily. "Because I'm Italian. They said it's a good thing I'm a citizen or they would send me to a detention camp."

"I'm sorry to hear this, Sandro."

"I have a friend, a guy who's not Italian, who might be able to take you there this afternoon. Give me your number there and wait and I'll ask him and call you back."

I looked through the glass of the door and saw Dennis and Ruthie with two large paper bags waiting for me.

I hung up and slid open the folding door. "My cousin's boat was impounded. He's asking a friend to help us find another boat."

The phone rang, so I closed the door and picked up. "You got lucky, Tony," Sandro said. "My friend Shelby can take you. I told him to gas up his boat. He's got one of those special permissions you need now to operate. He had to go to the Customhouse down there in the city to get it."

"I can meet him at the harbor, Sandro, thanks. What's the name of his boat?"

"It's the *Manchester Maiden*. Nothing fancy, but it'll get you there, and Shelby is a good man. I'll meet you there."

"I'll pay him for the gas. I know it's a precious commodity now, right?"

"Yeah, that's for sure. Hey, Tony, don't forget you have to get there and back before sunset!"

"What do you mean, Sandro?"

"Nobody can be out in Suisun Bay between sunset and sunrise. You know, the government has all these rules and regulations now. If they find you out after dark, they'll arrest you all, lock up Shelby's boat and he'll be mad at me."

"Well, I'd better get going then. At least we have the president's 'Pacific War Time' now so it'll stay light later. Thanks for helping out, *cugino mio. Ciao.*"

"*Prego, Dottore*! But don't get caught out on the water after dark."

Chapter 28   Friday, April 17, 1942

"Would you like me to drive, Tony?" Dennis asked, as we walked into the parking lot.

"So you enjoyed driving a *real* car when we went to Pescadero, eh?"

Dennis smiled. "I did enjoy that trip. The Century deserves its 'Bankers' Hot Rod' title. How about it?"

I slipped my keys out of my pocket and tossed them to Dennis. "We're in a hurry," I said, "but no hot-rodding, all right?"

"Aw, Tony. I like going fast," Ruthie said. "Let's see what you've got, Dennis."

Dennis got in the driver's seat, I took the passenger seat, and Ruthie got in the back. As the car warmed up, I took the roadmap out of the glove compartment and unfolded it.

"I think we should take Highway 24, not Highway 40." I looked over at Dennis. "Don't you agree?"

"It's a more direct route, and besides if we took 40 we'd have to fight all the traffic going to and from the shipyards in Richmond."

"Don't I get to decide?" Ruthie joked. "I'm the backseat driver, aren't I?"

Dennis laughed, put the car in gear, and we drove out of the parking lot. Midday traffic slowed us down until we got to Broadway. Then Dennis took advantage of our horsepower and we quickly made it out Broadway and through the new Broadway Tunnel.

"Wow," Ruthie exclaimed, as we exited the tunnel. "What's that huge mountain way out there?" We were on Highway 24 headed to Walnut Creek, and I guessed that, like so many San Franciscans, she'd never set foot in Contra Costa County.

"That's Mount Diablo," Dennis said. "My college is just a ways over there to the right, in Moraga."

"When we went through that tunnel, I thought we were in a nightmare. Dark. Scary. With the cars coming right at us so close, so fast, in the other lane. But now, all of a sudden, we're out here in the country. Beautiful sunshine. Miles and miles of trees and hills."

"They just opened the tunnel four years ago," I said. "Pretty soon people will be able to drive out here and they'll start building houses."

"Not as long as the war goes on," Dennis said.

It took us almost an hour to finish our forty mile trip from Mills College to Martinez. Dennis concentrated on passing every single car and truck we came to. I gave Dennis and Ruthie some background on Jake Oster. "He headed the Law and Order Committee after the bombing of the parade in favor of the British side back in 1916. The radicals all blamed him, and me, for the frame-up of Mooney and Billings for killing all those people. But it was the district attorney who framed those two socialists. We just organized a citizen's committee that supported the investigation! Jake and I believed that the terrorists were German agents trying to rattle everybody and discourage us from getting into World War I."

"Were you and Oster right about that?" Ruthie asked.

"Nobody knows for sure to this day who the real bomber was," I said, "but we know that Mooney and Billings didn't do it."

"So," Dennis said, "in Oster's mind, scaring the public with a fifth columnist stabbing a leading civil defense official would be like a saboteur scaring the public by bombing a patriotic parade back then."

We were pulling into the parking lot alongside the fishing boats at the harbor in Martinez.

"Right," I said. "If the public thought it was an Axis sympathizer who killed Winthrop, Christian and Mary Chen would be off the hook."

Ruthie said, "I still don't understand, Tony. Why would Oster *want* to cover up a self-defense killing by an innocent boy and a girl fighting off a kidnapper in the first place?"

"Good question, Ruthie, and that's why we need to hear what Jake has to say, so hold on to that thought, all right?"

We got out of the car, gathered up our sandwiches and drinks and walked toward the boats. Alessandro was standing next to a tall, thin, hard-looking man in his seventies. I waved to Sandro and he smiled and waved back.

I introduced Dennis and Ruthie and Sandro introduced us to his friend Shelby, whose craggy face was covered by a three or four day growth of black and gray whiskers.

Shelby didn't smile, but he helped Ruthie step over the railing into the boat like he was Sir Francis Drake and she was Queen Elizabeth. He told us to put on life jackets and showed us where to stand alongside the outrigger booms and the trawling nets in the stern. Sandro untied the boat, and we slowly sailed out of the harbor and into Suisun Bay. Shelby's daughter, a young version of himself, with long black hair tied back, wearing a denim jacket, was at the wheel.

"Your watches say 3:30, but it's 2:30 by the sun," Shelby shouted over the noise of the engine as we entered the open waters of the bay. "I don't know what you plan to do at the club, but whatever it is you need to be done by 5:30 at the latest. That'll give us time to get back to the harbor before sunset. If you're not back at the boat by 5:30, I'm leaving without you."

"Don't worry," I said, "that should be enough time. If we're late and you leave without us, all I'd ask is that you return for us tomorrow morning."

"*Dottore*, of course," Sandro replied. Shelby nodded, and left us to join his daughter in the wheelhouse.

Suisun Bay was filled with military and civilian craft. The water was relatively calm, with a strong current and a light wind. We ate our sandwiches. Sandro said, "Don't throw your bottles into the bay. Put them in that canvas bag over there."

Dennis went for a walk and almost fell several times when he lost his balance. In thirty minutes we were across the bay and tying up at the Marshall Island dock. I smiled, watching both Dennis and Ruthie wobbling a bit as they started to walk up the dock to the clubhouse. They were clearly not used to getting their sea legs and then going back to using their land legs afterwards.

I led Dennis and Ruthie into the office in the clubhouse and we went up to the counter. The caretaker was sitting behind a desk on the other side.

"Good afternoon, I'm Commissioner Bosco and these are my associates," I said to the grandmotherly-looking woman in her sixties. She got up from the desk and came to the counter.

"You look familiar, Commissioner, I'm Mabel Lemke. I remember your coming with Mr. Oster."

"You have a splendid memory," I replied. "Can you direct me to his cabin?"

She smiled in a good natured way. "He's one of only three guests we have now, and we put him in the Father Serra Cabin, his favorite. Can I make you folks some coffee?"

"Thank you, that would sure hit the spot," Ruthie said.

"I'll go get Jake and we'll come back and join you and Dennis here where we can talk," I said to Ruthie.

I left them in the dining room and walked forty yards through the grounds to the Father Serra, one of a dozen twelve by fifteen cabins scattered among the eucalyptus and oak trees. All built of redwood, they'd weathered into graying structures that complemented, rather than clashed with, the natural colors of the trees and the bushes.

I knocked on the door of the cabin. When nobody answered, I made a fist and pounded.

The door opened abruptly. A startled Jake Oster looked at me disbelievingly. He had bags under his eyes and his hair was uncombed.

"Tony, what in God's name are you doing here?"

"I'm here to ask you that very question, my old friend," I said. "I'm here with Detective Dennis Sullivan and my assistant Ruthie Fuller. We know about Mary and Christian killing Harlan Winthrop. We have questions about that and about what happened to his body. I think you moved his body to Coit Tower and I need you to explain to me why you did that."

The color had gone out of Jake's face. He looked deflated. "This is very irregular, Tony. How did you know I was here? Why are you involving yourself in this?"

"Chief O'Reilly has delegated us to investigate Winthrop's murder, Jake. Let's not make this any more uncomfortable than it already is. The caretaker is making coffee. Let's go sit down and discuss this like sensible people."

Chapter 29   Friday, April 17, 1942

The windows faced west and the dining room was filled with light. The bright spring sunshine nearly blinded me. I needed to get this over with and get back to the boat on time. We sat down around the table.

"Jake, you and I go way back, more than twenty-five years. To the Market Street bombing. We both went through hell and high water trying to find out who killed all those people. And we got it wrong."

Jake started to say something, but I cut him off.

"I need you to listen to me and then you can talk to us. "We know that Winthrop was killed in self-defense by Christian and Mary Chen, and I think you moved the body from his boat to Coit Tower. I'm here to hear your explanation and Dennis and Ruthie are here as witnesses, but it's time to own up and take responsibility, Jake."

Jake's whole body sagged and now I saw an old man sitting across from me. He leaned forward and put his head in his hands, saying nothing.

"We're old friends, and I respect and trust you, Jake. If that wasn't the case, you'd be in handcuffs right now and on the way to the city jail. I'm doing you a favor by even talking to you here, so show some respect back to me and cooperate, can you?"

Jake shook his head back and forth and groaned.

"I think you wanted to protect Mary and Christian, but you could have done that by calling the police from the Yacht Harbor."

Jake sat up and looked me in the eye, seeming to regain some composure.

"I think you decided to try and shift the blame to an individual or group involved in fifth column activity," I said. "But I want you to tell me what you did in your own words."

"Well," Jake said, "you're half right, Tony. When Louie and I got to Winthrop's boat, we were horrified. Then I had an idea. You and I always thought it was German agents, not two socialists that bombed Market Street in 1916. Remember?"

I nodded. "Yes, of course I remember."

"They killed forty people," he continued, "trying to scare the city into refusing to go to war against the Central Powers."

Dennis and Ruthie sat silently, spellbound by Jake's story.

"To this day," Jake said, "we don't know who really did that bombing, so I thought if I put the body in Coit Tower and made it look like an Axis sympathizer killed Winthrop, and the police could never find the killer, it would just turn into another unsolved crime like the one in 1916."

"You said Tony was half right," Ruthie said. "What's the other half?"

I couldn't help thinking that I wished Flora and I could have had children as bright as Ruthie.

Jake turned and looked at Ruthie. He smiled, seeming to regain some of his composure. "Well, young lady, I also thought that if the papers printed large headlines about a 'Fifth Column Murder in Coit Tower' maybe people would start behaving more responsibly about civil defense."

"Huh," Dennis said. "You're talking about that speech General DeWitt made in February about Mayor Rossi and the city government failing to properly protect the city."

"I think the general was right," Jake said. "Maybe he was wrong about Japanese planes flying over the city, but he sure was right about the larger point: people aren't being vigilant enough."

"Jake, that's a convoluted way of thinking for somebody of your experience," I said. "Plus, you're playing God here, deciding you have the right to possibly scare the devil out of thousands of people, rather than trust the police department to handle a case that was clearly self-defense."

"Afterwards, I did have second thoughts," Jake said, "but then it was too late. And when nothing appeared in the papers, I didn't know what to think."

"What I want to know," Ruthie said, "is why did you take Mary and Christian to Mills College?"

"Aurelia Reinhardt, the President of Mills, is an old dear friend," Jake said. "We went together by train to the Republican Party convention in '36. She is a person who is always ready to help out people who are at their wit's end.

"I drove them to the college and Aurelia arranged for Mary to study for her college degree in their brand new Modern Dance program. Christian will work there as a cook and he can finish his high school degree by correspondence. His eighteenth birthday is soon. When he gets his diploma, he'll enlist in the Navy."

Jake seemed revived. Perhaps getting this all off his chest had given him a boost. The sun was lower in the sky, not shining directly into my eyes now. I realized we should get back to the boat and start the trip back to the city.

"All right Jake, here's what's going to happen," I said. "We're not going to arrest you at this point. I can't promise we won't do so in the future. That will depend on what the chief says after we explain all of this to him."

"Can I stay here for now, Tony? You've put the fear of God in me. I feel better having told all of this to you, but I'm also conscious of what I knew all the time — I stepped over a line I shouldn't have crossed."

"You're right about that, Jake. I know that the chief wants to keep the murder quiet, especially the fact that the body was in Coit Tower. He wants it kept from the press and the public."

"Yes, stay here if you want," Dennis said, "but don't leave the bay area. We'll report to O'Reilly tomorrow and Tony will contact you about what the chief decides. We'll send a messenger since there's no telephone here."

"One more thing," I said to Jake as I got up from the table.

"What's that, Tony?" He remained sitting and looked up at me.

"I want you to make an appointment with a psychiatrist as soon as possible. You've been through a shocking experience and you don't seem yourself."

"Tony, I don't think—"

Dennis interrupted him. "Mr. Oster, we are doing you a big favor by allowing you to stay here. We could be arresting you on suspicion of aiding and abetting a murder. I suggest you listen to Tony and do what he says."

Oster nodded agreement and stayed quiet.

We all got up from the table and said goodbye to Mabel Lemke and Jake.

"Let's get back to the boat," I said.

Shelby started the engine of the *Manchester Maiden* as soon as we were on board. After we docked in Martinez I handed Shelby a ten-dollar bill and thanked him. He nodded, still unsmiling, and touched the brim of his captain's hat in a salute. "Anytime, Commissioner," he said.

I gave Sandro a bear hug, said goodbye and tossed the keys to Dennis.

"Ruthie, why don't you sit in front with Dennis? I'll be the back seat driver this time."

Chapter 30   Saturday, April 18, 1942

t a few minutes past 8:00, after a frittata and cappuccino, I kissed Flora goodbye and drove to Portsmouth Square. I parked in Charlie's garage and asked him to service my Century and to wash and polish it.

"Where've you been, Commissioner? Your car is never this dirty."

"It's a long story, Charlie. I'll tell you later. I've got a meeting with the chief now."

Dennis and Ruthie met me in the lobby, and we went upstairs to the chief's office.

"I'm glad to see you," Maggie said to me as we entered. She gave Ruthie's baseball cap a quizzical look.

"I was beginning to fear for your safety. He was grumbling yesterday about how he gave you forty-eight hours to clean up some mess and he hadn't heard from you. I'll let him know you're here."

"Ruthie," Maggie said, "are you sure you want to be wearing that San Francisco Seals baseball cap when you see the chief?"

She had worn it when we drove back to the city from Martinez. She'd enjoyed riding in front and had remarked about the views during the ride. When we got to the Bay Bridge, she'd rolled down her window to see the view of the city after we drove through the Yerba Buena Island tunnel.

"Aw, Maggie," she said now, "don't be a spoil sport. The chief knows me. I'm not worried."

The inside door opened, and a nearly bald man in his sixties wearing an Army officer's uniform with several rows of decorations came out. When he put on his hat, I recognized him as General DeWitt. The chief introduced us, the general said goodbye and went out.

"Well," said the chief, scowling, "I just sat through yet another meeting listening to the Army telling me how to run my department. The general there wants to fine tune every single minute of our Jap roundup operation next Tuesday. I tried to tell him that's not his job. Maybe one of these days, he'll get the message!"

"But, Ruthie," he said, leaning over to pick up a sheet of paper from his desk, "DeWitt has approved Tony's request to have your Commie friend and her Jap husband and their half-breed kid all go together to a detention center."

"Chief, that's great," Ruthie said. "But I sure wish you'd stop saying 'Jap' and 'Commie' all the time."

O'Reilly's eyes registered her complaint, but he ignored her and continued talking.

"The general is sending them all out into the desert at a place called Manzanar. He wasn't happy about it."

He turned to me. "Tony, I suggest you don't make a habit of these kinds of things. DeWitt doesn't like people trying to tell him how to do his job any more than I do."

He sat down and leaned back, motioning us to sit in the three chairs around his desk. "So what do you have to report?"

We told him the whole story, not sparing him Harlan Winthrop's little group of degenerates. Mary and Christian's killing Winthrop in self-defense. Jake Oster's cover up. Aurelia Reinhardt's well-intentioned participation.

"Chief," Dennis said, "I thought at first that Jake's story didn't make sense. But if we allow for him being elderly and too upset by what he found on the boat to think straight, then his behavior makes more sense."

"All right," the chief said. "Tony, tell Jake Oster I'm going to ignore what he did. I know him well, and I can turn a blind eye, especially if as you say he's had a nervous breakdown. Keeping our people calm and protecting them from fear is more important than slapping the wrist of an old man who took the law into his own hands for a good cause."

"He'll be glad to hear that, Chief."

Dennis had put the red ledger book on the chief's desk as I told the story, and now O'Reilly picked it up and looked at the names and addresses.

"Looking at the girl's names in the back of this book, I can see that some of them are missing person cases."

"Wow, really?" Ruthie exclaimed.

"Yes. You all know I've worked with Miss Donaldina Cameron, the woman from the Chinatown Mission. For years, she's worked with the police department to save girls from prostitution." He frowned and shook his head. "She came to me several times in the past couple of years and told me about girls who had disappeared. I see some of their names right here in this book.

"Miss Cameron found them good jobs as maids or housekeepers with families after they graduated from her Presbyterian Mission School in Chinatown. And then, suddenly, they disappeared from the face of the Earth. We figured they had been kidnapped and taken back into sex slavery, but we ran into a brick wall when we tried to trace what happened to them."

Ruthie said, "Chief, it looks like now you can arrest those men on that list and punish them for a whole bunch of crimes that we solved without even knowing we were doing it."

O'Reilly looked at Ruthie for several seconds, then said softly, "I'm sorry, Ruthie, but none of these men will be charged, let alone convicted. They are all 'leading citizens of our great city' as the papers would put it. If we were to issue warrants for their arrest, all hell would break loose, forgive my French."

"Also," Dennis said, "we have no evidence whatsoever that connects any of those individuals with any of those girls. The fact that their names are in a book is not enough to charge them, let alone arrest and convict them."

"The chief and Dennis are right, Ruthie," I said. "It's sad but true that some of the wealthiest and most powerful people in the city not only enjoy depraved activity, they profit from it, either directly or indirectly."

"And now that all these people are pouring into the city because of the war, the vice business will get even bigger," Dennis said. "I bet there will be more copies than ever printed of Jack Lord's little guidebook *How to Sin in San Francisco*. Somebody told me that the bookstores kept running out of copies and they had to reprint it five times!"

"What we can and will do," the chief said, "is impound the boat and the house in Sausalito. We will also impound the apartment on Nob Hill. His car, his boat, and all of the furnishings in his apartment will disappear just like he did. He will be cremated and his ashes dumped in the Bay. I have my ways of quietly putting out the word to those guys on the list that they would be better off if they just forget they ever knew anything about Harlan Winthrop and his little vice den."

"But, Chief," Ruthie said, a measure of distress in her voice, "shouldn't the people know what really happened?"

"This is San Francisco, Ruthie. The people who need to know already know," he replied.

Chapter 31   Tuesday, October 27, 1942

"Tony," Flora called up the stairs, "are you finished dressing? The brioche is ready and I'm making the cappuccino. We need to hurry or we will be late for the ceremony."

I finished tying my tie, a plaid of greens and blues that would go well with my dark grey autumn weight suit, and walked downstairs to the kitchen.

We sat down and had our breakfast. Flora said, "I have to admit, I don't at all miss your smoking, especially during our meals like this. I don't know if you notice the difference but the whole house is fresher since you stopped."

"What I notice," I said, "is that it feels like something is missing when I'm reading my *Chronicle* and drinking my first espresso of the day. And at times like last night, after we finished our meal at the Riviera Restaurant, and we were enjoying our after dinner drink. But other than times like that, I don't miss smoking at all."

"I felt bad for Ruthie last night," Flora said. "It must be so terrible for her, hearing that her cousin was killed on that awful Bataan Death March. Of course I haven't known her that long and I can't know what she was like before, but she seemed quite sociable considering what she's been through."

"Yes," I agreed, "but in some ways I think it's easier now for her. At least she knows that he died and she's not still living day to day wondering about his fate. What do you think, Flora?"

"I think it's hard to know. Only she knows what she is feeling. But I know if I was in that situation I would rather hold out hope for you than know you were dead!"

"Speaking of Ruthie, she and Dennis seem to get along very well, don't they," Flora continued. "I thought he was very attentive to her. He's such a nice young man!"

"They have probably gotten to know each other better because they are working on another special assignment for the chief," I said. "He asked them to work with the military police to keep track of the goings on at all those new bars and saloons that have opened up in the Mission and the Tenderloin. Now Ruthie is going undercover again, but this time she is going to bars and keeping her eyes and ears open for gambling and prostitution."

After we finished our breakfast, Flora cleaned up the kitchen and I answered a few letters in my study. I decided to wear my black Homburg today and my light topcoat. Flora put on her brown wool coat, suede shoes that matched, and a dark brown Clochard hat. As we got into my Buick Century, I said, "Flora, you will be the best dressed and most beautiful woman at the ceremony."

We drove to North Beach taking Union Street to Columbus Avenue. As we passed the new Stella Pastry shop, we saw Ruthie and Dennis going in the front door, so I parked and we walked across the street and greeted them. They both blushed when they saw us, but I smiled and said, "Fancy meeting you here."

"Well, long time no see," Ruthie replied and we all laughed. They bought cappuccino and brioche. We all sat together, chatting while they had their breakfast.

Afterwards, we walked up to Chinatown and headed for the Chinatown Telephone Exchange. The Police Department had blocked off Grant Avenue between Washington and Clay. A long, thin two-man Japanese submarine was mounted on a platform. It was captured at Pearl Harbor and moved to Grant Avenue for today's Navy Day ceremonies. The government had sent it around the country on a flatbed truck to show that we can defeat our enemies.

A small crowd had gathered for the ceremony. A Navy captain and a sailor, Chief O'Reilly, and Mayor Rossi were standing on a small platform built on the sidewalk across from it. Louie and Elizabeth Chen were also there, along with Jake and Mildred, Linette and her husband Alex Bassano, President Aurelia Reinhardt, and Mary Chen. We joined and greeted them all.

A group of a dozen boys stood at the end of the block. We saw an elderly Chinese man dressed in colorful silk Confucian priest's robes, who introduced himself as Dr. Henry Yee.

A small group of Chinese girls and boys walked up beating little drums, clashing small cymbals and slapping tambourines. Dr. Yee walked over to the submarine and threw little pieces of what looked like herbs toward the craft, making a statement in Chinese. "He's driving the Japanese devils out," said Louie Chen.

The boys who had been standing together down the block came over. They walked up a ladder on the other side, and lined up on the top of the sub facing us. Christian Chen led the little procession. The boys were mostly dressed in suits and ties but a few wore dungarees and wool jackets.

When the boys were all in place, the Navy captain walked up and asked them to recite after him their oath of enlistment in the United States Navy. Newspaper photographers recorded the event, their big boxy cameras clicking away.

Elizabeth Chen, and Mildred and Linette Oster were wiping tears from their eyes as we all said goodbye. Dennis, Flora and Jake Oster were chatting with Chief O'Reilly and the mayor. I noticed that President Reinhardt and Ruthie seemed to be having a serious discussion. I walked over to them and thanked the president again for helping Mary and Christian Chen survive and recover from their experience on Palm Sunday. "I'm so glad I was able to play a part in this horrible event having a positive outcome," she said.

"Guess what, Tony?" Ruthie said. "President Reinhardt has made me an offer! She says that since I have a degree in Russian from Berkeley, I ought to come and teach it to her girls at Mills College. What do you think? Should I do it?"

I smiled. "I think President Reinhardt knows a good thing when she sees it," I said. "Things are changing so quickly in our world. We're going to need a lot more leaders with personality, style, and intelligence who can speak Russian."

Epilogue   Sunday, November 8, 1942

irst they unfurled the flag and then they sang the song. They liked meeting in the clubhouse at Spreckels Lake, even though they knew the long dead German-American philanthropist would object to Nazi sympathizers meeting in a Golden Gate Park public building.

Jake Oster had attended these anniversary celebrations of the Munich Putsch since the time of the Friends of the New Germany. He'd not missed one, even when the German American Bund, several years later, met severe condemnation and fell into disrepute.

Now the Swastika flew over Paris, Vienna, Budapest, and Warsaw. The *Reich* controlled Western and Central Europe and West and North Africa.

Oster felt a warm glow inside as he reflected on the progress of the German people since Hitler became chancellor.

At the same time, the odds were against him and his American friends who stayed loyal to the *Reich*. Several dozen was a normal turnout before the Wehrmacht invaded Poland. But after that, people stopped coming, even though they changed their name to Bavarian Model Boat Club. Tonight only five of them had shown up.

At seventy-four, Jake was by far the oldest, and he'd become the informal leader of their social activities. Tonight, he felt a downbeat nervous energy in the room. After he passed around the bottles of Burgermeister and they all toasted "*Sieg Heil,*" they bemoaned the Allied success in North Africa. They all admitted to being worried about the Russian campaign.

After his second bottle of Burgermeister, Jake found himself talking with the two *Kameraden* who had helped him move the body of Harlan Winthrop from his boat to Coit Tower.

"I suppose we must consider the Coit Tower operation a failure," said the man in his sixties with a Friedrich Nietzsche mustache and a flushed face.

"We couldn't have foreseen that Chief O'Reilly and Tony Bosco could keep it out of the papers," replied the thin man in his fifties with black hair slicked back like Joseph Goebbels. "Nobody even knows that Winthrop was killed."

"On the other hand," Jake said, "nobody knows that we were involved in anything." He smiled coldly. "The war is far from over, gentlemen. There will be other opportunities to weaken morale and stir up fear and anxiety."

He signaled a toast, they clinked bottles, and the three of them shouted out, *"Ein Volk, Ein Reich, Ein Führer!"*

Acknowledgements and Author's Note

Mayor Angelo J. Rossi, Archbishop John J. Mitty, Mills College President Aurelia Reinhardt and the other real individuals, organizations, and institutions that are fictionalized in this novel were researched with the assistance of the ever helpful folks at the San Francisco History Center at the Main Public Library, the Labor Archives and Research Center of San Francisco State University, and the Chancery Archives of the Archdiocese of San Francisco. Thank you all, once again. I received valuable suggestions from Robert Cherny, Mary Claire Heffron, James Grusky Issel, Marjorie Penn Lasky, Diane M.T. North, Zeese Papanikolos, and Charles Wollenberg. Special thanks to my editor Andrei Cherascu, my copy editor Dj Hendrickson, and Chris Carlsson, who designed and published the book.

About the Author

Bill Issel, professor of history emeritus at San Francisco State University, is the author of *For Both Cross and Flag* (Temple, 2009), *Church and State in the City* (Temple, 2013), *Traitors* (Carleton Street, 2021), "Jews and Catholics Against Prejudice," in *California Jews* (Brandeis, 2003), and "Deutsche Einwanderer in San Francisco," in *California Dreams: San Francisco, Ein Porträt* (Bundeskunsthalle, 2019). He is the winner of the Distinguished Scholar Award of the American Catholic Historical Association, the Award of Merit of the San Francisco Historical Society, research and public history grants from the National Endowment of Humanities and the Rockefeller Foundation, and three Fulbright teaching grants, in London (1978-1979), Pécs (2008-2009), and Timişoara (2018-2019).

www.ingramcontent.com/pod-product-compliance
Lightning Source LLC
Chambersburg PA
CBHW051050050726
47592CB00002B/464